M000036513

THE SPEED
OF WATER

THE SPEED OF WATER

A NOVEL

JONATHAN WALLACH

Copyrighted Material

The Speed of Water

Copyright 2018 by Jonathan Wallach.
All Rights Reserved.

No part of this publication may be reproduced, stored in a retrieval system or transmitted, in any form or by any means—electronic, mechanical, photocopying, recording or otherwise—without prior written permission from the publisher, except for the inclusion of brief quotations in a review.

For information about this title or to order other books and/or electronic media, contact the publisher:

WaHi Productions, LLC
Jonathanwallach2@gmail.com

ISBNs:
Print: 978-1-7321967-0-4
eBook: 978-1-7321967-1-1

Library of Congress Control Number: 2018910929

Printed in the United States of America

Cover and Interior design: 1106 Design

"Treasure is measured in units of love
Which means you may find you are rich
Beyond your wildest dreams."
Above & Beyond, Treasure

I wish you were here to see this one, dad.
For my family.

CHAPTER I

The 7:30 out of Denver made a lazy turn into the moonlight and landed.

Michael Grand turned on his cell phone to discover that his dad had died during the flight.

Michael collected his things, hailed a taxi, and headed home. From the back of the cab, the drive over the mountains was illuminated by a full moon, and Michael was able to see the city lights reflecting off of the ocean. Traffic was worse than what Michael remembered, but he was lost in his thoughts; he didn't really remember the drive home. Michael's mom, Sarah, was waiting for him when he arrived. There was a light wind blowing off the water, which allowed the wind chimes to talk. Sarah had been crying; her face was red and puffy.

Michael hugged his mom, and both started crying. "Your dad loved you. He was always your biggest fan," said Sarah.

"I miss him."

"Your sister is coming in tomorrow, but your brother is somewhere in Afghanistan. I don't know if he can make it in time."

"It'll be okay. We'll be thinking of him," said Michael.

"How long are you staying?"

"Mom, I was starting a trial. I had to get a continuance. I can stay only a few days."

The Grand family had lived long enough in Hawaii to be considered *Kamaaina*. Michael's dad, Joshua, had been a State Appellate Court Judge, a Vietnam Veteran who served in the Brown Water Navy as a young Lieutenant, including two ferocious weeks in Hue during the 1968 Tet Offensive, which Joshua never talked about, despite winning the Navy Cross. After Vietnam, Joshua had attended law school at Berkeley, largely on the GI Bill. Joshua was the son of Holocaust survivors who met in a DP camp in Allied-occupied Germany in 1946 and fled the end of the world to paradise after the war had ended.

Joshua had been born in Hawaii, as were all of his kids. Sarah was a retired nurse. Michael's sister, Janice, was an orthopedic surgeon who was married to a radiologist and living in Denver with their two kids, in what established mental-health providers would have called an "unhappy marriage." Michael's brother, Isaac, was pure-blood Hawaiian and had been adopted by the Grand family when Isaac's dad, Joshua's first bailiff, died suddenly during a criminal trial.

Isaac's mother had died in childbirth. Isaac went to live with his abusive, alcoholic uncle. Joshua and Sarah ended that relationship and petitioned to adopt Isaac the day after his ninth birthday. It was common practice in the Hawaii of old to *hanai* a child—adopt or place a child into a childless family. Sometimes, a child would be *hanai'd* when it was given to the grandparents to raise. Joshua and Sarah cherished the generosity and unconditional love and respect inherit in this practice and wanted it to continue for Isaac. Isaac was currently a Navy SARC deployed in Afghanistan with the Marine Raider Regiment.

Michael Grand was a lawyer who'd moved to Atlanta six years ago. Michael and Janice were blood, but Michael and Isaac were more in tune as siblings. Isaac became the little brother, Michael the bigger brother, a role that, over time, he grew to adore.

Sarah was talking to Michael and said, "We have to meet the Rabbi tomorrow, go to the funeral home, and clean the house. Can you take me around tomorrow?"

"Sure." Michael, noticeably tired and upset, said, "I thought the doctors said he was going into the hospital for a few days and that he would be home by Thanksgiving."

His mom responded, "He was, Honey. That was the plan, but he was a lot sicker than any one of us thought. The cancer had spread to his spine, and he must have been in a lot of pain, but he never showed it."

"Mom, if I'd known that, I would have come out sooner."

"Your dad never wanted anyone to fuss about him."

"Mom, as soon as I got your call that he was in the hospital, I dropped everything. I was literally just starting a trial. I thought I had more time."

Sarah always had a way of calming her oldest son. She said, "I know, baby—we all did. He went so fast."

"I couldn't be there in the end. If I hadn't gotten stuck in traffic, I could have made it. If I'd gotten an earlier flight, I could have made it."

"Michael, don't beat yourself up. Your dad smiled when I told him you were coming in. It gave him the energy he needed to begin his long journey. He always knew that you loved him." Sarah stood up. "Are you hungry? There's some chicken in the fridge."

Michael, suddenly feeling tired said, "Nah, I ate on the plane. I'm beat. I'm going to bed."

"Alright, Honey. There are towels on your bed."

"Mom, are you going to be okay?"

"Yes, I just want to sit here for a bit. I'll see you in the morning."

Michael fell asleep as soon as he put his head on his pillow.

The winter-morning sun woke him. When Michael went out into the living room, he noticed that his mom had not moved from where she'd been last night.

"Mom, did you stay here all night?"

Sarah responded, "I couldn't sleep. The bed was so empty."

Michael said, "Mom, we have a lot to do. You need to get some rest."

"I'll be okay. Let me make breakfast. You must be hungry."

"Mom, I'll take care of it. What would you like?"

"I honestly don't have the energy for food."

"Mom, you need to eat. You need your energy. Let me fix you something."

Michael's mom didn't answer, so he went to the kitchen and cut some papaya, scrambled some eggs, made toast, and brewed a pot of coffee. Michael brought a plate over to his mom, and she ate a little.

Michael went outside with a cup of coffee and listened to the waves roll in. The house was old, built in the 1920s by some obscure writer who'd sold one trashy novel, cashed out, and moved to Hawaii, but it was only footsteps away from the ocean. The house had survived a dozen hurricanes over the years and at least three ornery teenagers. Joshua and Sarah loved the house since they'd seen it one day in 1973. It was run down and had been, briefly, a hippie commune before it was abandoned, but Joshua saw that it had potential. It had a half-acre front yard with mango, banana, and palm trees spread out. Sarah remembered seeing it for the first time late in the day and loved the way that the light played off of the house. It started out as a bungalow, but over time, subsequent owners had added to it. Joshua and Sarah added the *mauka* wing when Isaac was adopted, adding two extra bedrooms, one of which became Joshua's study. There was a wrap-around lanai that started in the front of the house and went to the rear, where Michael was sitting in a weathered Adirondack chair.

CHAPTER 2

It started raining, and Michael always loved watching the way that the rain and ocean would seem to merge on the horizon. Somewhere, a gecko was talking. Sarah came out wrapped in an old quilt and holding a cup of coffee.

"Your father loved this house."

When Joshua and Sarah had bought the house in the early 1970s, it was all they could afford. While all their friends told them to move to the more affluent Kahala area to be closer to work and the beautiful people, Joshua and Sarah fell in love with Kailua, the sleepy little town on the windward side of Oahu. Over time, as Japanese, then Korean, then Chinese investors decided to start buying Hawaii, the little house became very valuable. Joshua had gotten a kick out of the time when some Japanese guy pulled up in front of the house in a black limo and went to talk to Joshua, who was mowing the grass in the front yard. The guy opened a briefcase full of money and told Joshua he wanted to buy the house. Joshua demurred, as he would many times over the years when the same kind of offer presented itself.

Over time, the neighbors all got the bug, though, and sold their tiny little houses on the beach to investors, actors, foreign nationals, anyone with cash, and the little houses were all slowly torn down and replaced by huge mansions. The Grand house was the one of the few remaining remnants of when Hawaii was a different, simpler place.

"I loved this house, too. It was a great place to grow up."

"We should get going. We have a busy day."

"Mom, can we take dad's car?"

"I don't think there's any gas in it. Your father drove it a few days before he went into the hospital and said that it was empty."

"We can stop in town and get some gas."

The car was a sky-blue 1969 280SL Pagode Series, which sat next to Sarah's Volvo, with the NPR and Clinton-Gore bumper stickers on the rear window. Joshua had paid $5000 for it years ago when a Navy buddy needed some cash. The car had been one of his favorite possessions. Aside from 154,000 original miles on the speedometer, the car was in good condition. Joshua was always meticulous with his things. It was just as Michael had remembered. The "My son and my money both go to Boston University" license-plate holder that Michael had given to his dad when he first came home as a freshman from college—along with the worn US Navy bumper sticker—were still there. Michael got into the driver's seat and rubbed the massive leather steering wheel. Sarah got in and sat in the passenger seat.

"Dad loved this fucking car. A lot of memories in this car. I learned to drive in it. Dad made me learn to drive on it so that I could learn how to drive a stick."

Sarah sat there silently.

"I remember when grandpa flipped out when he got it—told him he wasn't welcome in his house. I must have been nine or ten."

"Your grandpa didn't have much love for Germans back then."

Michael's grandfather, born Moshe Gradlewicz in Lodz, Poland, was old enough to remember the ghetto before he was sent to Auschwitz as a young man. Through inner strength that rarely befalls a 20-year-old, Moshe survived the camps when his entire family did not. As a boy before the war, Moshe remembered watching an old, grainy movie of Duke Kahanamoku surfing and told his mother that he would move to Hawaii one day. When he immigrated to the United States with his new bride in 1946, he changed the family name to "Grand" to sound "more American."

When Moshe met Ruth, it was love at first sight. They were married when they were still in the DP camp. They were both 22. Moshe opened a small tailor shop in Kailua. His father had been a tailor, and Moshe had worked in his father's store, where the elder taught the young boy everything he knew. Moshe was a quick study and quickly began to work alongside his father. Ruth worked the books and handled the cash register. Joshua came a year later. Together, they earned enough to raise Joshua, buy a house, send Joshua to college, and try to build upon a life that had almost been extinguished before it began.

"Still, I always loved this car." On the way, Michael drove past the building that had housed the tailor shop. A fast-food restaurant now occupied the space. "Mom, when did that happen?" Michael said as he pointed to the restaurant, which was packed with people.

"Three years ago. It used to make your dad very sad. He refused to go in there."

"I would have figured dad would have told me about that."

"He didn't like to tell many people about it, Michael."

CHAPTER 3

The drive into Honolulu from Kailua always struck Michael as enchanting. For the most part, the Pali Highway was a two-lane road on the side of a mountain with a view of most of the island below, including an endless coastline. The road was curvy enough to be fun on dark, moonlit nights, and as a teenager, he would take his dad's car up the Pali and try to go as fast as he could, especially through the tunnel. Michael always drove with his shoes off. He loved the way the pedals felt on his toes. It was perfectly acceptable to drive without shoes in Hawaii, legal even. When Michael had taken his driving test, the tester asked him, "Shoes or no shoes?" Michael chose "no shoes."

Sometimes, late at night, when there were no other drivers out, Michael would drive in the middle of the road. There were several times when the police had caught him at this. In those days, the police wouldn't arrest you. They would take you home to your dad at 3 AM. This made for a different class of kids growing up in Hawaii, as they all had a healthy respect for law enforcement. It was always interesting when that happened to Michael, as his dad was a State

Circuit Court judge at the time. The cops would bang on the door, and Joshua would invite them in for coffee. They would tell Joshua about their families, as most of the cops knew most of the judges back then. They would go to each other's baby luaus, know the names of their kids, and watch them all grow up.

Joshua always thought of creative ways to punish Michael when this happened. Once, after Michael got pulled over for speeding in his dad's car, he locked Michael in the garage overnight and made him sleep in the car but would secretly sneak out hourly to make sure that everything was okay. The next morning, Michael discovered that the door was never actually locked. That was Michael's dad.

Michael and Sarah met with the family trust attorney, and Michael discovered that his parents had named him a trustee of their trust. The lawyer indicated that Joshua had made some smart investments over the years. Years ago, one of Joshua's physician friends convinced Joshua to invest in a biotech start-up. The company turned out to be one of the most profitable in history. Joshua had left Sarah with more than enough money for Sarah to be comfortable for the rest of her life. In addition, Sarah would receive Joshua's State of Hawaii civil-servant pension, which was well funded after almost 30 years of contributions.

Michael reviewed the will and discovered that the 280SL was his, along with the old Rolex GMT that Joshua had worn since Sarah had bought it for him in Hong Kong when they were both there during R&R in 1967. Joshua's collection of shotguns was to be divided between Michael and Isaac. Joshua wanted Isaac to have the 1970 Harley Davidson Panhead that Isaac had convinced his dad to get and that they worked on. The bike terrified Joshua, but he couldn't get rid of it because Isaac would get upset. It sat un-ridden in the corner of the garage for years.

Janice got the stamp and rare-coin collections, which she and her dad had spent hours on. One day, after a chemo treatment, Joshua had the coin collection appraised. The appraiser was shocked to see American Revolutionary War and Roman coins in such pristine shape and valued the collection at more than $400,000.

The old fishing boat, house, and cabin on Kauai were to be put in the revocable family trust to be used and shared among the family. All other property remaining after Sarah's death would be divided equally between Michael, Janice, and Isaac. During the meeting, Michael had to excuse himself because he started feeling dizzy, and all he could hear was the sound of his heart beating in his ears. He ran to the bathroom to vomit, but nothing came up. He tried to cry, but no tears came. He wound up sitting on the toilet for a minute to catch his breath and regain his composure. He went back to the meeting.

Afterwards, they went to the funeral home and dropped off Joshua's favorite suit, shirt, tie, and shoes.

"It's fitting that dad gets to spend eternity in a Brioni suit. Man, he loved this suit. He bought it when he visited me a few years ago. We went to the ABA convention in San Francisco together. We spent five hours in Neiman Marcus shopping for ties."

Sarah went in to look at Joshua, see him for the last time.

Michael didn't have the stomach to follow, so he waited outside.

Sarah came out about twenty minutes later and said that he looked very peaceful. Her phone rang. It was the Governor's Chief of Staff asking if arrangements for a public viewing had been made. Sarah told him that they were working on the funeral arrangements as they spoke and were waiting for her daughter to fly in from the mainland. They needed to honor Jewish Law and bury Joshua prior to sundown that Friday. The Governor's Chief of Staff told Sarah that the Governor had ordered all state flags to fly at half-mast in honor of Joshua.

"Mom, let me deal with all of these people."

"It's okay, Honey. These plans were set in motion when your dad first got sick. These are actually his plans. He figured everything out. He didn't want me to worry about any of this."

Janice texted Michael to tell him that her plane had landed in San Francisco and that she would be in around 9 PM. Michael told her that he would pick her up.

As they drove from downtown, Michael began to notice more high-rises in the distance than he ever saw in the past. "Mom, when did those come?"

"Oh, within the past two to three years. Your dad used to say that Honolulu was beginning to look like 'fucking Hong Kong.'"

As they got closer, Michael could see why. "Wow, this is where Isaac and I used to cut class to go surfing. Now it's a condo. Last night, when I came in, I noticed how bad the traffic was. It was bad before, but now, it's kind of stupid—it's the middle of the day."

"You haven't been back in a while, Honey. It's been like this for a long time. Even sleepy little Kailua has bad traffic now. It sometimes takes 30 minutes to get from downtown Kailua to the house."

"Wow! I used to ride my bike down there in 10 minutes."

"That building over there sold out all of its million-dollar-plus units in a day, even before the building was constructed. That's the new Hawaii."

"I think I like the old Hawaii better."

"That's something your father would have said."

CHAPTER 4

Michael dropped his mom off at home to rest before the rabbi came over. He went into Kailua town and grabbed some lemongrass chicken sandwiches, summer rolls, and iced espresso with condensed milk from a Vietnamese takeout place. He also stopped at Hawaiian Island Creations to buy some t-shirts, surf trunks, and black flip-flops, as he didn't have time to pack these when he'd left Atlanta. He stopped by a supermarket to buy some *poke* and Hinano beer, which he missed in Atlanta. Although *poke* was becoming ubiquitous on the mainland, it wasn't the same as eating *poke* made out of fish that might have been caught the previous day. Michael remembered fishing with his dad and Isaac once when Joshua hooked a big *Ahi*, brought it up onto the boat, bled it, cut out a huge piece of flesh, and immediately made *poke*. The three of them ate it right there. It was incredible.

As Michael pulled out of the parking lot, he saw the flashing blue-and-red lights of a Honolulu Police Department cruiser behind him. As he pulled over, he heard a voice say over the loudspeaker,

"*Haole* boy, pull your dad's car to the side of the road and do as I say, or I'll tase your white ass, brah!"

Michael knew this voice, although he hadn't heard it in a while. Billy Kawashita. Michael and Billy had gone to middle school and high school together. Billy, Isaac, and Michael were thick as thieves when they were younger and were inseparable. Michael got out of the car, and Billy gave him a big bear hug.

"Mike, when did you get in?"

"Last night. Man, you look good!"

"Sorry about your dad. We all loved him."

"Thanks. He loved working with you guys. How are Kimberly and the kids?"

"Jack is 15, and Ryan is 13, and I think they will try to kill each other."

"Wow! I remember going to their first-year baby luaus. Man, I feel really old."

"How's your mom doing? Does she need anything?"

"I think she's in shock. They were married for almost fifty years."

"I'll stop by later and help you drink all that beer and eat all of your *poke*."

"I would love that."

The rabbi was there when Michael returned. He shook Michael's hand and gave him a hug. "Your dad was a great man. Everyone loved him. I will come up with some nice words to say about him."

"Thank you."

"Try not to beat yourselves up. In the Jewish tradition of *Kriah*, Jews would tear their clothes in an expression of grief and sorrow. This would also tell others that something was not quite right and that the rest of us should treat them with a little deference. We don't really tear our clothes anymore, but we do use these." The rabbi gave Michael and Sarah a piece of cut black cloth in a safety pin. "Feel free to wear these. They might give you some comfort. We will sit *Shiva* after the funeral. Sarah, have you figured out when the funeral will be?"

"They think it will be the day after tomorrow, Thursday. We're trying to arrange with the Governor's Office, and the Navy wants to send an honor guard."

"Michael, can you offer a eulogy for your dad?"

"I would be honored."

Michael went to lie in his bed and listened to the wind and rain. He thought how he used to love falling asleep to that sound. Next thing he knew, his mom was knocking on his door to tell him that Billy had arrived.

Sarah had watched both men grow up and was particularly fond of Billy. Billy's mom and Sarah were nurses together at Queen's.

Billy and Michael went out on the front lanai and watched the rain come down. Both had beers and a bowl of *poke* in their hands.

Billy asked, "Remember that time when you and I tried to scare your dad by sneaking up behind the house and banging on the back window?"

"Yep—we scared the shit out of my mom instead, and she chased us out to the front yard screaming at us and holding her frying pan, telling us that she was going to 'fucking kill us both.' Good times."

Billy said, "How is Atlanta? Kimberly and I want to come visit."

"Atlanta is fine."

"Are you still banging that hot drug rep?"

"Nah, she told me that I have commitment issues."

Billy giggled.

"I'm currently not seeing anyone. Work is too crazy."

"Mike, you never had any trouble with the ladies. Even Kimberly fell under your spell. You should be beating them off with a stick."

"I am kind of past that stage in my life, Billy."

Billy told Michael, "I hear your doctor is still in town. Kimberly saw her last week at *Shirokiya*."

Michael took in a long, deep breath and took a second to reply. "Diana and I were a long time ago, and besides, she cheated on me, and last I heard, she married the guy."

Billy could sense his friend's pain but also knew there was something else there. "No, brahddah. She bailed on him."

"Billy, how did you hear that?"

"I have my sources."

Michael sat back in the Adirondack chair and took a large swig of his Hinano bottle. "Well, Diana was six years ago. I have long ago moved on."

"Okey dokey—if you say so. Kimberly and I thought you were pretty great together."

Michael playfully defaulted to his trial-lawyer self. "Objection,—badgering the witness."

Billy changed the subject. "Is your brother coming to the funeral?"

"Nah. He's in Afghanistan somewhere."

"I heard he made Senior Chief."

"Yep. My dad took time off from work to fly to Pendleton when he heard. He was thrilled. That was before he got sick. It was the last time they saw each other—a year ago."

"Did you go?"

"No, I was in trial."

"How did that go for you?"

"I lost."

"Yeah, you did."

"I sense the sarcasm in your voice."

"Mike, how many times did you see your old man in the past year, or when he got sick?"

"Twice."

"Look, brah. I know Atlanta is a long way away and you're crazy busy, but don't you think that you might have missed out on seeing your dad?"

"Billy, as soon as I heard that he was in the hospital, I dropped everything. Literally. My admin came running into court when I was performing *voir dire* and told me that my mom was calling me every ten minutes to tell me that Dad had gone into the hospital. I ran home to throw a few things in a bag and got the earliest flight out. I didn't make it. I flew all day, and he still died before I landed. How do you think that makes me feel?"

"Mike, I'm sorry. I get it, but we all saw your dad getting sicker and sicker. He still liked to talk to the old cops in the courthouse that he knew from when he was a trial judge. He refused to stop working as long as he was able to do so. All the cops who worked with him loved him. Everyone rallied around him. You missed all of that."

Billy Kawashita was an old soul at 45, fourth-generation Japanese in Hawaii. Billy's great-grandfather had been brought to Hawaii from Japan in the early 1900s to help pick sugarcane. Billy's grandfather and father were both cops. The idea of caring for his elders, including dropping everything for them, had been ingrained in his DNA. Like so many other children in Hawaii, Billy still lived in the same house he grew up in. As his parents became more elderly, he and Kimberly would care for them, cook for them, take them on family outings. Billy's kids loved their grandparents.

"It wasn't by choice, Bill. I thought that I had more time."

"We all did, brah. We all did. He went fast. It wasn't even six months. Mike, how long are you here for?"

"Until next Thursday."

Billy got up. "Thanks for the beers. I have to get home to Kimberly and the kids. I'll see you on Thursday."

"'Night, Bill."

"'Night, Mike."

CHAPTER 5

Michael picked up Janice in the 280SL. The rain had stopped a few hours earlier, and Michael put the top down for the drive up over the Pali. He loved the roar of the wind in his ears as he sped toward the tunnel. As a kid, when his father let him take his car, he would lower the top, race up the road, and then downshift only when he cleared the tunnels, entered the Honolulu side of the road, and hit the Oahu Country Club. Tonight, Michael did the same thing, making a quick run of the Pali Highway. There were other, more direct routes to the airport, but Michael loved the way the 280SL handled the curves of the road, how he could hammer the straights, even downhill and in the rain, making the brakes work in unison with the shifting. For Michael, cars were empirical and tactile. He loved the sight, smell, and sound of driving. Every day on the road was different. Some days you get to test yourself. Some days you just learn.

For Michael, driving wasn't just about muscle, boost, and horse-power—it was about the *feel* of the car and the road. Driving was one of the few hobbies that Michael loved because he would focus only on the small window of the road in front of him, which then consumed and focused his thoughts. When Michael couldn't sleep or was anxious about a case, he would drive. Michael knew that he was a car guy since he'd been a kid. He would get terrible earaches, and the only way that Joshua could calm him down was to put him in the car and drive. Even at 2 AM when Michael would wake up screaming, Joshua would buckle him into the passenger seat of the 280SL and drive for hours until Michael quieted down and fell asleep. Joshua would usually take his young son to a diner at sunrise for breakfast, where Michael would make friends with all of the vampire workers, the third-shifters, the truck drivers, the prostitutes, and police officers getting in a meal before their day either started or ended.

As Michael pulled up to the arrivals area, Janice was already waiting for him with her luggage. She was on the phone talking to her husband. Michael got out of the car, and he and Janice hugged.

"How was the flight?"

"Bumpy, and a kid was kicking my seatback the entire way from San Francisco."

"How long are you staying?"

"Until Sunday. Michael, what about you?"

"I go back next Thursday."

They got in the car, and Michael drove off. Other than when Janice asked to stop at a 24-hour pharmacy to get some toiletries, they didn't speak on the way home. When Michael pulled the car into the driveway, they saw that the lights were still on in the house, meaning that their mom was probably still awake. They found Sarah on the couch, asleep under a quilt with the TV on softly. Sarah woke up when they called her name. She sat up and immediately got up and ran to Janice to give her a big hug, while grabbing hold of Michael as they all hugged together in silence.

"Your dad loved you kids. He always said that you three were what made him the proudest."

Janice started crying.

Michael stood there for a minute and then excused himself to go and write his father's eulogy. He also needed desperately to check in with his office and thought it was weird that he hadn't touched his cell phone since Janice texted him in San Francisco. Hawaii, the house, the beach, the water, all had that effect on him. Wherever he was in the world, he always came home to recharge his batteries, as no other place on Earth could do this for him. But over time, when he went away to school and came back, Hawaii was changing for him. A lot of the beauty was gone; a lot of his friends had left for better opportunities on the mainland, as he had done. Those who'd stayed, people like Billy Kawashita, knew that they could never leave. When he'd left Hawaii six years prior, Michael told himself that he would never come back, even though he'd been born there and loved the place.

Michael went into his dad's study and stood in front of the desk. There were lots of fond memories in this study. Michael remembered from his childhood the stacks of case-law books that would be piled on the desk, written in what seemed to be a foreign language. He loved trying to read through them. Once, his dad found Michael asleep with his head on an open *Hawaii Reporter* filled with new cases, and Joshua knew right then and there that his son would one day become an attorney.

As Michael looked around the room, it was exactly how he remembered it. Next to a reproduction of the United States Constitution, there was a small, square frame with a crudely assembled felt yellow star that had "*Juden*" stamped in the middle. It was Moshe's badge, used to stigmatize, isolate, and control the Jews during the Nazi reign. He was forced to wear it for so many years. For some reason, he kept it. Joshua found it after he was cleaning out his parents' apartment when Ruth died. The badge was in an old cigar box in the safe near the kitchen. Joshua was astonished to find it. He never knew it was there. His parents never talked about what had happened to them during World War II. Joshua kept the yellow star next to the Constitution. It was his of saying that protecting and defending the Constitution would be a future deterrent to Yellow Stars. Michael looked at the walls filled with the important artifacts of his dad's life.

There was an antique, framed, hand-written English contract beginning with the words "This Indenture" written prominently at the top hanging behind Joshua's chair. There was a framed twenty-dollar overprint next to the indenture. Joshua had gotten it years ago from a coin shop in Ala Moana Center. Overprints were issued to the then-Territory of Hawaii during World War II to distinguish the currency from others in circulation, in case Hawaii was ever captured by the Japanese. The serial numbers were in red, with a black "HAWAII" stamped on the back. There was a framed wood sign that read "Don't tell my mother I am a lawyer. She thinks I work at the local bordello." Michael had given it to his father years ago. There were family photos on Joshua's desk of the kids and Sarah during various points in their lives.

Michael pushed "Play" on his dad's Bose CD player. The sounds of a Bach piano cantata filled the room. *Of course*, Michael thought. Joshua had always loved to work to Bach. Michael sat at his father's desk. As Michael listened, he wrote what he could and then went out to the living room. Janice and Sarah were talking on the couch. Michael said that he was exhausted and bid them both "Goodnight." Michael climbed into bed, opened the window, and immediately fell asleep listening to the gentle sound of the surf.

CHAPTER 6

The limo came to the house early. Sarah had been up since dawn, calling and making sure that all of the funeral arrangements had been made. The Grands had opted for a graveside service at the family plot, with a small reception at the house to follow. Joshua could have been buried at Punchbowl, the famous military cemetery where the unidentified killed on December 7, 1941, along with Ernie Pyle and Ellison Onizuka, the humble Hawaii-born astronaut who was aboard the *Challenger* when it exploded shortly after liftoff on January 28, 1986, were interred, but it meant that Sarah could not be buried with him. In the end, Joshua wanted to be buried next to his mom and dad. The family plot in an old Chinese cemetery in Manoa had been selected by Moshe because he thought it was the most beautiful location on the island. There was a very old, established Chinese community in Manoa, the by-product of some long-ago social order that prescribed where who would live.

The Governor spoke about sacrifice, honor, service, and the incredible man that was Joshua Grand. The Chief Justice and the Chief of Police also spoke about how they were honored to be Joshua's friend. Michael gave a beautiful eulogy honoring an exceptional man who was his father. He told of his dad always being his counselor, even after many years of being a successful lawyer, and how his dad was always there for him. Michael spoke of how when he was in law school, Joshua would call him every night and go over cases with him that he had learned about that day. This tradition continued when Michael became a lawyer and the two would meet on most Fridays for lunch in Chinatown and go over cases that each were working on. Michael said it was like being able to sit down with God and talk about Genesis, how his father had one of the best legal minds he'd ever known. Michael said that the world was a better place with his dad in it. Sarah and Janice sobbed in the front row. A Navy honor guard presented Sarah with a folded American flag on behalf of a grateful nation.

The rabbi said that Jews believe that when a person is born, the angels weep, but when they die and return, the angels rejoice and that they would definitely be rejoicing when Joshua arrived, that he was a *Mensch* in every sense of the word. Even the rain showed up for a time to pay tribute but then receded, and the sun came out. The rabbi led the mourners in the *Kaddish*, a Hebrew prayer that speaks to the living about the dead. It was then and there that Michael Grand realized that, up to that point, the mourner's *Kaddish* had been a largely abstract construct. Of course, he'd said it for his grandparents when they died, but he was very young at the time. It didn't really mean anything to him. He had said it many times during Friday night *Shabbat* services for the six million who died in the Holocaust, but that didn't really relate to him. Saying the *Kaddish* for a parent, though—that hit home. He immediately felt connected to his loved ones.

The service concluded, and the family led the procession of hundreds of people to the Grand family plot, where Joshua's coffin was lying next to an open hole. Joshua Grand loved nice things, but he was also a modest man. In the end, Sarah opted for a simple coffin with a Star of David engraved on the lid, thinking it would be the perfect tribute to her husband. Typically, Jews do not believe in giving flowers when someone dies, but Sarah wanted some beauty, so she placed a triple-strand orchid lei around the Star of David on the top of Joshua's coffin.

Everyone proceeded to the coffin, and as it was lowered, one by one, people threw a handful of dirt on the coffin from a big, damp pile of dirt next to grave. You can't live on a small island for more than seventy years and not know anybody. Joshua Grand knew everybody. His family used to call him "*The Mayor.*" He would often be found in the hall of the courthouse talking to anybody. The family would go to Costco, and Joshua would find a dozen people he knew, most of whom he would talk to for several minutes. Joshua used to teach Criminal Law at the law school. The only way that a student could get an "A" in his class was to name the janitors who worked in the building. Joshua did this not only because he talked to the janitors and would even invite them home for dinner on occasion, but more importantly, to instill in the young lawyers-to-be that it was essential to know and recognize "the little people in life." It seemed like everyone on Oahu showed up for Joshua Grand's funeral. Joshua's funeral was aired as a segment on the evening's local news channels.

After the graveside service, Sarah, Michael, and Janice stood and dutifully greeted everyone as they formed a line and thanked them for honoring Joshua. Michael thought it seemed like an eternity, and he started to experience a tightness in his chest, so he excused himself to sit down. From the corner of his eye, he saw a person approach. She was wearing a Navy Dress Uniform. It was Diana Eisenberg. Anyone who was watching the scene would have noticed an attractive 40-something blonde in a Navy uniform walking up to a handsome 40-something man wearing a nice suit and holding an open umbrella over his head.

"Hello, Diana."

"Hello, Michael. I came to say 'Goodbye' to your dad. He always treated me like a member of the family."

Michael's heart starting beating harder. Diana was the very last person he wanted to see on this day. "I see that you got your fourth stripe. It was what you always wanted." Diana had recently been awarded the rank of US Navy Captain.

"It's good to see you, Michael. How long are you in town?"

"I thought that doctors were supposed to know the danger of opening old wounds."

"Look, Michael. I didn't come here to fight with you. I came here to honor your dad. I have to get back to work. It was nice seeing you."

It was nice seeing you too, thought Michael. At that moment, Michael realized that it was a long time since he'd had that thought.

Sarah saw that Michael was talking to Diana, and she came up and gave Diana a big hug. They both started crying.

Diana and Michael had a long history. They knew each other before either started their life arc, when things were a lot less complicated. Diana grew up on the East Coast to socialist-leaning liberal Jews. Her dad was a television repairman; her mom worked in a department store selling perfume. Her mom died when she was 14, and her dad raised her as best as he could but often didn't know what to do with his brilliant, precocious daughter. Diana had a full academic scholarship to Boston University.

Michael met Diana when she was studying in the library and he was talking loudly with his friends. She thought he was obnoxious, but he thought she was smoking hot, and he asked her out. Diana laughed at him, got up, and left. Every night, Michael would go back to the same spot in the library, hoping to see her again. He waited a month. Then, on one Friday night, when every other student was at some crazy party or another, Diana showed up and saw that Michael was the only person sitting at the table. They started talking. They wound up dating on and off in college. Diana would usually spend summers in Hawaii with the Grands, starting her second year at Boston University. They were always seen everywhere, and people always told them that they made a great couple.

One brisk October morning after an early morning run along the Charles River before classes, Michael stopped at the BU boathouse to watch the rowing crews enter the water, something he loved to do. Michael had a moment of clarity. *One day, I am going to marry Diana. She's the one.* When Diana got into Columbia for medical school but her dad was unable to pay the tuition, she joined the Navy. Michael's grades were not good enough to follow her, so he went to law school in Denver. They tried long-distance dating and would fly to visit each other on long breaks, but the distance between them eventually was the worst jealous mistress, and they wound up growing distant, then apart, and then parted ways altogether.

It wasn't until Michael had returned to Hawaii to practice law and had moved back home that he ran into Diana while food shopping. Michael was grabbing items for dinner, and he walked up and saw a woman from behind in a tan Navy uniform. *She looks like a woman I once knew*, Michael thought. Diana had stayed in the Navy to pay for med school, and they'd sent her to Pearl Harbor when she finished her critical-care residency at Bethesda. Michael had no idea that Diana was even on the Island, let alone that he would ever see her again. Diana was going to call the Grand house and inquire into Michael's whereabouts but ran into him before she would ever pick up the phone. Twenty minutes after they saw each other, they were naked on Diana's couch. Diana was at the Grand house on most weekends. Sarah and Joshua loved her. Sarah told Diana to come to the house for the evening *Shiva* later, and Michael stared at his mother.

The rain had started again when the limo pulled up to the Grand house. People had already gathered and brought food. On the kitchen table was food typical of a celebration of any kind, Hawaii-style, including a celebration of life. There was *poke*, cooked prawns, *chow fun*, roasted duck with dumplings, sushi, King's Bakery sweet bread, teriyaki chicken, *Kal Bi*, *Lomi Lomi*, *manapua*, *malasadas*, *Haupia*, chicken long rice, banana bread, beef broccoli, *Char Siu*. In Hawaii, even a Jewish funeral has *Char Siu*. Michael and Janice were mingling with people. Sarah was on the couch talking to an old friend. The house was full of people wishing to pay their tributes to Joshua. The noise in the house was starting to agitate Michael, so he went out to the rear lanai with a beer to watch the rain, which was really starting to come down hard. Billy followed. The two of them just sat there, watching the choppy surf come onto the beach. Michael clinked the tip of Billy's beer bottle.

Janice came out later and plopped down next to Michael. "I'm beat. Long day." Billy and Janice were friendly growing up, but Janice was three years older and always told everyone that she was the smartest person in the family. She probably was. College at Stanford, medical school and residency at Duke, Janice was an exceptional physician and had her dad's work ethic. She rarely turned down a case. Billy used to call her "Jan-nice" growing up to irk her, and it usually worked.

"How's life, Jan-nice?" This time it didn't really bother her; she laughed when she remembered the name. "Things are good. I have a nice life." Answered with the typical cold, clinical precision that all but defined Janice. Janice's husband Dan was a nice enough guy but always seemed too busy at work or working out or skiing to really pay Michael any attention when they visited. He was the perfect husband for Janice.

"Hey, Bill. Remember the time that we all went to the drive-in with my mom and dad? We were in my mom's station wagon that you used to call the "brown fucker," and my dad drove off with the speaker still attached to the window."

Billy responded, "I do remember that. We saw *Battlestar Galactica* and could not hear anything because we were all stuffed in the back of the wagon, and your mom was screaming because she didn't like when there were explosions. Janice ate too many red vines, and she barfed."

"I didn't barf—I got a stomach ache and ran to the restroom."

Billy said, "That drive-in is now a private school. Before the school was built, I used to bust kids who would go up there and smoke *pakalolo* because they thought that they wouldn't get caught.

Janice chimed in and said, "Speaking about *pakalolo*, do you know where we can get some?"

Michael responded, "Janice, you did not just ask Sergeant Kawashita where we can find some marijuana!"

"Just asking. I thought it would be fun to smoke some to remind us of the days when we used to all do things like that."

Michael chimed in, "I haven't smoked pot since before law school. I stopped when it gave me hives."

Janice continued, "Remember when dad busted us for smoking pot in my bedroom?"

"Yep," Michael said. "He called in his buddy, the chief of police, who read us the riot act and told us that if we wanted to smoke pot, we had to do it outside."

"Different time. Cops were different then," said Janice.

Billy responded, "No, cops are still the same—we just have different priorities. I could care less if someone wants to smoke *pakalolo*. Seriously. With *Batu*, black-tar heroin, Chinese X that is laced with Fentanyl, I don't have time to chase kids who want to smoke weed." Billy continued, "We arrested a guy last week in Waimanalo. He was seriously beating his two-year-old to death. That kid would have died if there were any more beatings. I saw his boot print on his kid's chest. The kid had a fractured skull and old broken-rib injuries that had healed incorrectly. Closest I ever came to wanting to take a suspect in the back of my car and beat him to death. We deal with stuff like that, now, we don't deal with *pakalolo*."

Michael added, "I have defended my share of kids who have ruined their lives smoking pot. Most tend to be lower income. Once these kids get in the system, they never seem to get out."

Billy said, "We still have our share of that here, too. It hasn't really gone away. Your dad always seemed to take care to give hard sentences only to those kids who most deserved it. He didn't like it when they would take advantage of him or show up repeatedly in his courtroom." Billy continued, "Hey, Mike. What was the name of that kid? You defended him on a PCS. He was on remand—the one your dad said he would release if he could recite the Declaration of Independence?"

Michael responded. "Ikaika Collins."

"Yeah, *that kid*. You kept whispering the words to him, and he still couldn't get it."

Michael smiled at the memory.

Janice said, "That was our dad. He was good at trying to teach lessons."

Michael, drinking his beer, said, "Man, the one thing I miss is his voice. He used to call me all the time. We would talk about cases. We would talk about life. I could tell when he was in his chambers. He would always echo and talk softly because the other judges could hear his booming voice in their chambers, and they would complain." Michael turned to Janice and said, "Janice, do you remember what his voice sounded like?"

Janice said, "Sort of. I just talked to him about a week ago. I remember pieces in context, but I can't remember what his voice sounded like, either. I hope I get that back."

Kimberly came out and brought Michael another beer but told Billy that they had to get home to the kids.

"How come he gets another beer?" Billy asked his wife.

Kimberly said, "He's in mourning, and you have an early morning—remember?"

Billy got up. "Sigh. Yes, dear. Mike, I'll see you around. Let's do something before you go. Bye, Jan-nice. Nice seeing you again."

"You, too." Janice responded.

Michael got up to hug Billy and Kimberly. He saw his mom standing in the living room, talking to some guests who were still there. Sarah had a tired expression on her face. Michael said to his sister, "Hey, Janice. Did you bring any pharmaceuticals with you?"

Janice said, "Ambien—why?"

"Check out mom."

Janice turned around in the Adirondack chair and looked through one of the slits and saw Sarah. "Yeah, she looks exhausted. I'll go talk to her."

Janice got up, and Michael sat down to finish the beer that Kimberly had brought him, and he heard his sister talking to Diana.

Diana came out with a plate of food and two beers. She was still wearing her Navy dress uniform. "Is this seat taken?"

Michael beckoned with his hand to sit in the chair next to him. Michael said, "I am too tired to argue with you. Be my guest."

"You have my heartfelt condolences, Michael."

"Thank you."

Diana continued, "My dad died three years ago."

"Oh, I didn't know that. I'm sorry, Diana."

Diana looked at Michael and said, "I know what you're going through."

Michael took the beer out of Diana's outstretched hand and said, "You have no idea what I'm going through. I lost my rock."

Diana looked at Michael while balancing the plate of food on her knee. She looked at Michael and said, "You have joined the club of people who have lost their dads. Unfortunately, membership always grows."

Michael, exhausted from the day, said, "If you are going to be out here, can't you just sit here in silence and listen to the rain?"

Diana responded, "I just want to say one thing, Michael. Then I'll leave. I'm sorry the way things worked out between us six years ago. I was confused."

Michael said, "'*Confused*'? I was fucking in love with you, and I come home and find you in bed with that *proctologist*."

Diana interrupted Michael. "Urologist."

Michael continued. "Whatever. I found you in bed with that asshole, and my whole world ended. Why did you do it?"

"Michael, I was scared of losing you, but I didn't want to be confined, I wanted to get to Captain, and the only way I could see doing that was by working. I knew that would mean a deployment and that we would grow distant again, like when we tried dating when we were both in different cities. I didn't want to lose you."

"Well, Captain—you lost me. You're the reason I moved away. I moved as far away from you as I could find."

"I know that now. It took me a long time to figure that out." Diana started crying and continued talking. "I am not with him anymore. He asked me to marry him, and I said 'Yes.' We were engaged for a while, but in the end, he was busy, and I was busy, and I got deployed, and we just sort of ran out of gas. We weren't good for each other. I gave the ring back."

Michael responded, slowly. "I have had many, many beers, and I just buried my dad, so I'm not exactly thinking clearly now. But what do you want from me, Diana?"

"Can we start small? Can we be friends? Can I take you out to lunch tomorrow?"

"Diana, I don't think that's a good idea."

Diana started crying again.

Both of them just sat there and listened to the rain.

At some point, the rain stopped, and Michael fell asleep. Diana got up and left. Michael stayed outside and slept, listening to the gentle sound of the surf.

CHAPTER 7

Shortly after the sun rose the next morning, Michael woke up to his mom screaming. He ran inside and came face to face with his brother. Isaac Grand had traveled a long distance to stay for a very short time. Isaac was standing in the living room, wearing his fatigues and combat boots. He had a long beard flecked with gray. *A Taliban beard.* He saw his mom and sister hugging him.

Isaac and Michael had a bond that very few are fortunate to share. They were only three years apart and in the same family, but they were different. Michael was the "smart" one. Isaac was the "superior athlete." When Isaac came to live with the Grands, he was having trouble with his grades and was getting kicked out of various schools for fighting. Michael's parents made Michael watch over Isaac and take him everywhere. Initially, Michael did not like the arrangement, but Joshua and Sarah insisted and made the two of them sleep in the same room for a while. Eventually, they warmed to each other and became brothers.

Both Isaac and Michael spoke a mix of English, pidgin Hawaiian, and Yiddish growing up. Joshua and Sarah threw all kinds of resources at Isaac—private tutors, private school. Over time, these helped, and Isaac was able to matriculate through school, but he was never a standout student. Isaac could play any sport well, and Michael was the class clown. Both were very popular. Michael always helped Isaac with his homework and did his class projects for him. Isaac's teachers all knew this, but they all loved Michael and wanted Isaac to succeed when so many others in his shoes had not.

Isaac had this inner place built like a brick wall that few ever could match. He was an incredible swimmer, surfed all the time, could hold his breath for more than five minutes, and was the strongest and toughest kid around. After one kid in the 10th grade called Michael ". . . a fat Jew . . ." when Isaac was in the 8th grade, Isaac took the kid behind the gym and broke his jaw in four places, despite the kid being three years older than him. Joshua threw both Isaac and Michael into Aikido after that happened. Michael got a black belt, but Isaac got his second and third degrees in the same amount of time. Isaac basically spent the latter part of his high school years always fighting some kid who thought they could beat him in a fight. Back then, kids with an issue would go behind the gym after school and "go beef." The gym teachers would always be there, making sure that the fight never lasted long or really got out of hand. They would call the fight after one kid bloodied the other, would make them shake hands, and that was that. It was a different time. Isaac never lost any fight he was in during those years. Isaac had smarts that were not quantifiable by any school test.

When the kids were in their early teens, Sarah took them all in for aptitude testing. Janice was off the charts, Michael was incredibly smart, although he had trouble applying himself, but Isaac scored well, too, which shocked but did not surprise Sarah. Sarah always told Isaac that he could do anything that he applied himself to. Both went to college, but college wasn't really Isaac's thing, and he dropped out after two years to work as a welder, much to the dismay of his parents. Secretly, though, Sarah was thrilled to have Isaac home, under the same roof.

Michael was in his first year of law school on September 11th, 2001. The next day, Isaac joined the Navy and became a corpsman. When Michael was in law school, he "figured everything out" when he went through Constitutional Law in his second year. He told his dad that he knew what he was put on this earth to do—that was to help people who needed criminal representation. Isaac Grand figured everything out when his commanding officer gave him an opportunity to become a SARC. SARCs are special Navy Corpsmen. They receive all of the training given to the special operations Marine Force Recon units, are trained in amphibious entry, combat diving, parachute entry, small-unit tactics, deep reconnaissance, and direct action. In addition, SARCs are provided advanced dive medicine and 18-D Green Beret medic battlefield-trauma training. Isaac excelled at all of these standards. When Isaac made Senior Chief, he became his Team Leader. His men loved him, and he loved them. Isaac was currently on his fourth tour in Afghanistan.

"Holy shit!" Michael ran over to his brother and gave him a huge bear hug. "What are you doing here? I thought you were in Afghanistan."

"Um, yeah. *Yesterday* I was in Afghanistan. That was a long fucking flight, even with Ambien. I have a 72-hour leave."

Sarah said, "It makes my heart sing to have all of my kids in one place."

Isaac went into the kitchen and found all of the leftovers from the night before and proceeded to make the biggest plate of food his mother had ever seen. "Isaac, you always had a great appetite, but that is a huge plate of food."

"I am a growing boy, mom," Isaac responded.

Michael came in and got some *poke* out of the fridge and fried it for breakfast.

Janice went for a walk on the beach, and then came in and ate some cold *chow fun*, something she'd loved to do ever since she'd been a child.

Sarah made some coffee.

Isaac starting talking. "I'm sorry I couldn't get here sooner. I didn't even know Dad had gone into the hospital until they told me he had died."

Michael said, "Same here. As soon as I found out Dad was in the hospital, I came out. I didn't get here in time to see him in the hospital."

"Boys, don't beat yourselves up about this. Your father knew that you both loved him."

"*Easier said than done,*" Michael and Isaac said, almost in unison.

Isaac continued, "He was always there for me. I think he secretly cheered when I went into the Navy."

Sarah chimed in, "You were his Navy guy. Michael, you were his lawyer. Janice, you were his little girl who could do anything that she wanted to do. He saw that in you when you were four years old. He was proud of all of you. You were what made him the happiest."

Janice started to tear up. They all went into the living room, Michael opened the sliding doors so that they could hear the rain and surf, grabbed his iPod, and connected it to the Bose wave machine that was sitting on the mantel. He selected Gabby Pahanui, and *Leahi* came on. They all sat there in silence, taking in the moment. For the first time in more than ten years, the Grands had a family meal together.

CHAPTER 8

Michael hadn't checked his phone in two days and decided to call his office. He thought it was funny how indispensable his phone was a week ago and that now he could care less. He scrolled through his email. Most of it wasn't related to anything important. Michael had received a week-long continuance for his manslaughter trail. He was representing some rich kid who crashed his dad's Porsche while drunk and killed an elderly man walking across the street and then fled the scene. The kid fired his lawyer on the eve of his trial, and his father had called Michael. Michael never complained about his clients. He prided himself on the notion that everyone deserves a fair trial, and he dutifully represented what he called the "*dreck*" for 15 years. But this kid was getting to him a little. The kid had no remorse for what he did. When Michael met with his client for the first time, the kid looked Michael straight in his eyes and said, "You *are* going to get me off, right?" Maybe it was best that Michael had received a continuance on this one. He needed a little break from his client.

Michael's cell phone rang. It was Diana. Michael got up and went to his bedroom and let it ring for two rings, not sure if he wanted to answer it. In the end, he relented. "Good morning."

"Hi! How did you sleep?"

"I slept out on the lanai."

"You looked very peaceful when I left. I didn't want you to wake you, so I put the quilt on you."

"Thanks for that. Isaac surprised everyone. He just came home."

"Oh, that's great. I'm working up at Tripler today. He should stop by. There are still some nurses working here who would want to see him."

Isaac had worked at Tripler Army Medical Center for two years before he went off and became a SARC, and, during that time, he'd become very friendly with the female employees.

Diana said, "I'm finishing early, and then I am heading back to Kailua. Do you want to grab some dinner?"

"You're persistent, Dr. Eisenberg. What makes you think that I want to have anything to do with you?"

"Michael, it's just dinner."

"Let me think about it. Call me later, and I'll give you a decision."

Diana sighed. "Okay—that works. Talk to you later."

Michael hung up the phone, left it on his bed, and walked into the living room.

Isaac and Janice were out on the lanai, talking about trauma medicine. Sarah chimed in, "Mike, I am going to be an obnoxious Jewish Mother here, so let an old lady rant a little bit."

"Mom, please."

"Hang on Michael—let me finish. I would do anything not to see my babies suffer, and I know Diana caused you some pain, but I honestly don't think that she meant to hurt you."

"Mom, I came home and found her in bed with that guy."

"Honey, we have been through all of that a million times. You have to move on. She did. She's no longer seeing him. Your dad tried to teach you how to forgive. It was one of his best qualities. He never really stayed very mad at anyone for a long time."

"Mom, I can forgive her. A few years ago, I was sitting in some bar in Buckhead, and I literally remember the moment that I forgave Diana. I can forgive her, but I can't *forget*."

"That's up to you, Michael, but don't go through life with any regret. Regret can be very destructive. I think Diana still cares about you, and you two have a lot of shared history." Michael said to his mom, "I told her I would think about dinner. I didn't say 'No.' Let me think about it."

Billy came over to go surfing with Isaac. Isaac had called Billy from the cab and told him that he was in town for only a short time but wanted to go surfing. There was an early winter swell that was charging up and down the North Shore, and Sunset, Pipeline, and Waimea were blowing up with big waves. Billy, Michael, and Isaac all grew up surfing the waves in Hawaii; they knew that a ten-foot Hawaiian wave was really a twenty-foot wave anywhere else in the world.

Michael didn't surf much anymore, but Billy and Isaac surfed whenever they had the opportunity. Every beach house in Hawaii has at least one surfboard leaning against an outside wall, and there were several surfboards in various sizes at the Grand house, the impressive trophy collection amassed by Isaac and Michael over the years. Isaac took the old 10'2" Bear that he and Michael got at a garage sale for $50 and shared over the years; he put it in the back of Billy's F-150. They drove the hour or so drive to find surfing paradise. In the winter, swells along the North Shore could get as high as 20 feet plus. Billy was excited to be able to surf with Isaac again, after a few years.

Isaac was the kind of surfer who could still shred on a huge, old board. When Isaac surfed, people would come out to watch, because he did things on a surfboard that not many people could do. He turned down a chance to go pro because he didn't want his dad to think that he had become a surf bum. Isaac surfed wherever the Navy would send him. Once, he found some crazy waves in Diego Garcia, when Isaac was on ship in a task force that had stopped through on the way to the Persian Gulf. Even though it was forbidden to surf there and some British sailors had told him that, if he surfed there, the poisonous sea snakes would swim up and bite him in the balls, Isaac still scrounged for a surfboard and surfed in the middle of the night. Isaac was fearless.

Once, Isaac and Billy cut school to go surf some obscure break off of the Marine Base in Kaneohe. It was an Air Station then, and they paddled three or four miles from the reef off of Kailua beach and went around to the side of the island that was restricted to only military personnel. They found the break. Isaac later said it was "epic"; it was right below the final approach of the runway, and Marine F-4 Phantoms would come screaming in a few feet above their heads while they were surfing or waiting for surf in the lineup. Marines on the beach would clap when Isaac would tube or would do some aerial maneuvers. Isaac got tired and paddled to the beach, where the commanding general of the base had his house. Isaac walked up to his front door, rang the bell, and was immediately arrested by a half-dozen MPs. The MPs called Joshua, and he told them to keep his kid in the brig until he was able to extricate him later that day.

CHAPTER 9

Michael was reading his email, and Sarah and Janice were on the couch, looking at family photos, when Isaac and Billy walked in a few hours later.

Sarah said, "Billy Kawashita, I have told you a million times—do not track sand into my house."

"Sorry, Mrs. Grand."

"You are a grown man with grown children, and I have known you your entire life. You don't need to call me 'Mrs. Grand.'"

"Okay, Mrs. Grand."

Sarah said, "How was the surfing, boys?"

Isaac said, "We drove out to the North Shore. We could see the surf from the cane fields; they were coming in at 10–15 feet. Everything was pretty blown out, so we surfed for a bit; Then we went to *Kua'aina* for lunch and came home."

Michael said, "That doesn't sound like much fun."

Isaac responded, "It's way better than being in Helmand Province."

Michael responded, "True story, brother."

In the end, Michael decided to go out to dinner with Diana. He showered, put on a pair of jeans, borrowed one of his dad's Reyn Spooners, sprayed on his dad's cologne, and took the 280SL out to pick up Diana.

He found her sitting on the front porch of her house wearing a pretty floral-patterned dress that nicely accentuated her figure. She and Michael were the same age, but Diana looked ten years younger, as she obsessively worked out four times a week and watched everything she ate. They embraced, and Diana kissed him on the cheek.

"That's some dress, sailor."

Diana said, "You smell like your dad."

Michael said, "I borrowed his shirt and his cologne. Armani Aqua di Gio. He would only wear Aqua di Gio."

"Smells good."

Michael said, "Where do you want to go?"

Diana responded, "How about that Thai place you always liked and tried to get me to eat new things, but in the end, I would only eat their *Pad Thai*?"

Michael said, "*Saeng's*? Is that place still around?"

"It is, counselor. I go by it all the time, and I see it, but I haven't been in there in years."

"Why?" Michael asked.

"Because it reminded me of you."

Michael responded, "Well, then you need a corrective emotional experience, *Saeng's* it is."

Diana said, playfully, "I must say that you are rather cheerful."

Michael responded, "This is just dinner, right? And besides, I need something to take my mind off of the past few days."

"Just dinner, it is, counselor."

Dinner was enjoyable. They ordered a bottle of *Riesling, Pad Thai, green papaya salad,* mixed seafood curry, sticky rice. Michael looked around at the other diners. They appeared to be mostly tourists, including one loud table with two couples who were obviously a more than a little happy drinking *Singha* beer. The wine came. Michael tasted it, smelled the cork, and declared to the server that it was yummy. He raised a glass. "Thank you for helping me to celebrate my dad's life."

Diana raised her glass. "It was my great honor. It was the very least I could do. Your dad was a great man."

They caught up on their lives from where they'd left off six years ago. Michael admitted to Diana—the first time that he'd publicly told anyone—that he was burnt out in his job. Diana told him that she missed him all the time. Michael told Diana that he missed her as well. They finished the bottle of wine, ordered some banana tapioca pudding to split, paid the check, and left.

Michael drove the 280SL up to end of the road in Lanikai. He turned the car around, and they sat in the dark, listening to the sound of the ocean. Diana reached over and kissed Michael. Michael kissed her back.

Diana looked at Michael and asked him, "Do you want to come home with me?"

Michael responded, "Let's take it slow—okay?"

Diana said, "Sure. I'm off tomorrow. Do you want to do something?"

Michael said, "I was going to go paddle boarding at sunrise tomorrow. Want to come with? You can borrow Isaac's board."

Diana responded, "I would love to. If I can't wake up to see you, at least I can see you first thing in the morning."

"Deal."

Michael drove Diana home, and they made out a little in her driveway. Then Diana got out, and Michael backed the 280SL up and drove home.

CHAPTER 10

Michael got up at sunrise and threw on a pair of surf trunks. He walked by Isaac's room, and he could hear his brother loudly snoring behind the closed door. "Holy shit—he's going to stop breathing! I'm surprised he's not rattling the photos off of the wall!" Michael said out loud.

Sarah was in the kitchen, making coffee. Michael kissed the top of Sarah's head.

"How are you, mom?"

"I'm okay, Honey. How are you? How was your date last night?"

"It was good, Diana is coming over in a little bit. We're going paddle boarding."

"Go easy on her, Michael. She is trying to redeem herself."

"I know, mom. I am trying. I still love her, you know."

"I know you do."

"I just don't want to get hurt again."

"Michael, you have always told me that you have to go with the universe, let the current take you, surrender. You have always excelled at going with the flow. You should listen to the universe here and see where it takes you, here and now."

At that moment, Diana walked in, wearing a Peacemaker Trading Company t-shirt, board shorts, and black flip-flops.

Sarah kissed Diana on the cheek. "Good morning, sweetheart."

"Good morning, Sarah."

Michael saw the trademark buffalo on Diana's t-shirt and asked, "What is 'Peacemaker Trading Company'?"

Diana said, "A really cool company run by some great people."

Michael walked out the rear doors in the living room onto the patio and around to the side of the house, where the surfboards were stored next to the outside shower that is ubiquitous in all Hawaii beach homes. He put his sunglasses on as he went outside. Diana followed him out.

Michael grabbed Isaac's paddleboard and handed it to Diana. Michael said, "Here—this is a great board. Isaac did the Molokai Channel on this board." He grabbed his paddleboard and the two paddles and walked down to the beach with Diana. He took off his t-shirt and threw it into the sand by the beach access.

Diana kicked off her flip-flops and stripped off the board shorts and t-shirt, revealing a high-cut, black two-piece bikini that accented her tanned figure.

Michael got a good look at Diana in her bikini. "That is some outfit, sailor. You still got it."

"You don't look so bad yourself." Diana said, eyeing Michael's well-toned abdomen.

Michael pushed his paddleboard out, quickly dove into the cool water, swam to the board, and climbed on. Diana waded out to where she was waist deep in the ocean and climbed up on her board. Michael started paddling out to "The Mokes," about two miles away. The Mokes, or the Mokulua Islands, are two Islands about a mile off of Lanikai. They have been a famous backdrop for many movies and television shows filmed in Hawaii and are much loved by the residents of Kailua and Lanikai. Diana followed.

They paddled for an hour and a half, made their way around both islands, and paddled toward Lanikai beach. From there, they paddled back to Kailua beach. The mid-morning walkers, walkers with dogs, and the occasional fisherman were all out enjoying the beautiful morning.

Michael got down, sat on his board, and kicked his feet in the water. Diana paddled up beside him and sat down on her board. Michael leaned over and kissed Diana. Diana kissed him back and said, "Good workout—I'm sweating." They sat there for a few minutes, holding hands.

"This is nice."

"Sure is."

They paddled back, got dressed, and dropped the boards off at the house. Michael drove them to Starbucks. They sat outside with their coffee and blueberry oatcakes.

"Michael, I know I made a huge mistake, but I was shocked when I heard that you'd moved away so fast. You never do anything impulsive, and you pulling up the tent stakes so quickly and moving to Atlanta was so not like you." She could tell Michael was deep in thought.

Michael answered her. "I had to leave. Without you, the island was getting very small. I was getting *rock fever*. I had to do something. My parents wanted me to stay. Isaac wanted me to stay. Billy wanted me to stay. They all told me that I would find someone else. I didn't want someone else. I wanted you, and you broke my heart. My job didn't feel the same anymore. I stopped sleeping."

Diana started crying. Michael reached over and grabbed for Diana's hand. "I don't want to go through that again."

Diana said, "Neither do I. I don't want anyone but you. I learned that the hard way." Diana stopped crying.

They sat in silence and finished their coffees. Michael stood up and said, "Let's go."

Diana asked, "Where are we going?"

"Come on, come on. Let's go."

"You are so bossy, counselor. Where are we going?"

Michael responded, "We are going on a little field trip."

Michael drove Diana home. He said, "Grab some exercise gear, running shoes, water hydration, protein bars, and an outfit to go out in afterwards. I will pick you up in 45 minutes."

Diana giggled. "Okay—*mysterious*. I always liked that about you."

They kissed, and Michael drove off.

Forty-five minutes later, Diana was waiting for Michael in front of her house. "Where are we going?"

"You'll see."

Michael drove the long way into Honolulu and pulled into the park in Diamond Head Crater. "Good choice, I haven't been up here in a while," Diana said.

Michael grabbed a picnic basket out of the trunk of the car, and they shared a light lunch made for them by Sarah, who even put two homemade brownies in a plastic container and drew hearts on the napkins.

It was mid-afternoon when they started to climb the many steps to the top of Diamond Head. They passed other hikers, both going and coming, and when they weren't holding on to the railing or letting other hikers pass, they were holding hands. From the top of the Diamond Head, they had a 360-degree view of the entire island.

"I love it up here."

"Me, too. I don't see this view out of my condo in Atlanta. My dad used to like coming up here."

"Do you think I could come visit you in Atlanta? You say when, and I'll come out."

"I would like that."

Michael and Diana stood there in silence for what seemed like hours, just staring out at the infinite blue of the Pacific Ocean. Michael held Diana's hand; she rested her head on Michael's shoulder.

CHAPTER 11

The late-afternoon sun was heading lower into the sky when they started on their way down. When they finished, there were not many cars left in the parking lot. Michael went into the trunk of the 280SL and got out a towel, a pair of jeans, and one of his dad's aloha shirts. He wrapped the towel around his waist, and like anyone growing up in Hawaii knew how to do, he pulled down his shorts and replaced them with a pair of jeans in such a way as not to expose himself.

Diana watched him. "I have always loved when you did that. Even in Boston, you made it look like you were so cool."

"I was so cool. It took you months to figure that out."

"I didn't like you at first, if you remember, but you eventually wore me down with your boyish charm."

"Am I wearing you down now?"

"We'll see."

"Come on—I thought all you Navy girls were easy."

Diana stood up and said, "We are. As cool as you do that trick with your towel, I am not as gifted in that department. I am going to go change in the bathroom over there." Diana grabbed her things and set off for the park restroom.

Michael put on the aloha shirt and smelled it. It smelled like his dad. He put on his dad's watch and a pair of black Gucci loafers, no socks, and Diana walked back to the car, wearing a low-cut blue dress.

"You clean up well."

"Best I could do. That bathroom is really gross."

"You look great." They kissed.

Michael put the top down on the 280SL and drove into Waikiki. The late-afternoon sun reflected off of the windshield. He pulled into the front of the Halekulani hotel, and the valet guys ran out to open their car doors. Michael grabbed Diana's hand as they walked to House Without a Key just in time to catch the beginning of a fantastic sunset. Michael had called ahead and had a table reserved, with an unobstructed view of the water. The hostess had gone to high school with Michael, and they caught up for a minute.

When they were seated, Diana said, "Do you know everyone here?"

"No, that was my dad. A lot of the people I grew up with are long gone. Some stayed; I run into them from time to time."

They ordered wine and some appetizers and listened to the live Hawaiian music playing. They watched the pretty hula dancers dancing to the music. The sun was setting down past the horizon.

"Pretty nice moment."

"I'm so glad we were able to re-connect, Michael. You don't know how happy this makes me feel."

"You and I have a lot of history."

"Yes."

"Some really good. Some really bad."

"Don't rub my nose in it."

"I'm not."

"We were mostly good."

"Yes."

"How come we never wound up together? This is a question that I have been asking myself every day since I saw you at your dad's funeral. I was stupid."

Michael sighed and said, "I think it's a bit more nuanced than that. 'Stupid' is one thing I have never accused you of."

Diana continued, "I was confused. I didn't know what I wanted."

"What changed, Diana?"

"You. You came back into my life after I pretty much wrecked us." Diana started to tear up.

Michael held up his wine glass. "To you."

Diana picked up her wine glass. "To you."

Diana said to Michael, staring at him across the table, "Are you willing to give me another chance?"

Michael, with a wry grin, said. "Maybe."

They finished their dinner and left when the stars started to twinkle in the sky.

Michael drove the 280SL up over the Pali highway; Diana fell asleep in the passenger seat. Every time they stopped at a stoplight before entering the tunnels, Michael would glance over at Diana and watch her sleep. She looked so content. The rest of the drive, Michael listened to the drone of the engine and became lost in his thoughts.

Diana woke up just as Michael was driving into Kailua town. She smiled at him.

"How did you sleep?"

"Like a baby."

Michael pulled into Diana's driveway.

"Do you want to come in?"

"Yes."

Twenty minutes later, they were naked on Diana's couch. Afterwards, Diana and Michael were entwined in Diana's bed. Diana poked Michael in the ribs and said, "I thought that we were *taking it slow!*"

"Yeah—so did I. It was that fucking bikini. You did a Jedi mind trick on me with that bikini."

Diana giggled. They fell asleep in each other's arms for the first time in a long time.

CHAPTER 12

Diana and Michael woke up the next morning. They snuggled for a while, and then Diana got out of bed, showered, and got ready for work. Michael invited her over to the house for dinner late that night, and she accepted. Diana kissed him and left. Michael drove home. Isaac was sitting at the table, eating cereal out of one of Sarah's huge mixing bowls.

Michael said to Isaac, "That is a Jethro Bodine-sized breakfast."

Sarah and Janice had gone off to walk the beach together. Isaac looked at Michael, winked, and said, "Did you get laid?"

Michael sheepishly nodded.

"Yes! That's my boy!" and he high-fived Michael.

Billy was off for the day, so he came over. The first thing Isaac told him was that "Michael *schtupped* Diana!"

Billy was exuberant. "I knew it! I knew it! I knew you two still had something. Kimberly is going to be thrilled!" Billy high-fived Michael.

Michael sighed and said, "Great—now the whole fucking island is going to know in a matter of a few hours." Michael was always amazed at how that happened. He once saw a married buddy at the

San Francisco airport with a woman who was most definitely not his wife, and within a few hours of the plane landing, the entire island seemed to know that he was having an affair. The guy wound up getting into a messy divorce.

Sarah and Janice walked in, holding hands, and Sarah asked if anyone was hungry. It didn't matter that everyone had just eaten. Sarah took it upon herself to cook up a huge plate of eggs and pancakes. Everyone sat around and ate.

Janice said, "Billy, this reminds me of all the times that you would come over for dinner and we would sit around the table and talk."

Billy said, "I remember those days. I remember how much milk was on the table—there was always four or five gallons."

Sarah said, "True! We always had so many people at the table."

Billy continued, "I remember the bird, too. That thing really freaked me out. It used to imitate me. It would scream 'MRS. GRAND, MRS GRAND!!!!' and you would come running out. That damn bird would start bouncing up and down and laughing."

Everyone around the table starting laughing. They all remembered the parrot that Joshua had brought home. The kids were in their early teens. The parrot's name was "The Captain" and was apparently more than 75 years old and owned by a retired Navy Captain friend of Joshua's who could no longer care for it. Besides mimicking Billy, The Captain would mimic the kids and would swear like a sailor. Every morning at dawn, The Captain would scream, "WAKE UP, MOTHER FUCKERS!!!!" It got so bad that Sarah would leave the bird's cage covered until everyone got up. He would still curse. Joshua loved that parrot. Sarah did not. After a few years, one day the parrot was not to be found. Sarah said that it had died overnight and that she'd wrapped it in aluminum foil and threw it down the storm drain. The kids always thought that she opened his cage and let him fly away. Joshua was crushed.

Sarah was happy to have everyone around the table. Her children were a wonderful distraction, but she knew that, when the kids left, the house would become very sad and lonely.

Janice wanted to go to Waikiki, since it was her last day on Oahu, and she'd promised her kids that she would bring them some trinkets. Sarah said that she would like an outing, so they climbed into Sarah's Volvo and headed into Honolulu.

Michael was checking his email on the couch, and Isaac said to him, "Brah, do you bring that thing into the bathroom when you shit, too?"

"Sometimes."

Billy started laughing.

Isaac continued, "Brah, that is sick and wrong."

Michael didn't deny his brother's accusations. He tossed the phone on the couch and said, "I've been pretty good. I haven't checked it that much."

Isaac said, "*Oy Gevalt*! You're in Hawaii! You shouldn't be checking it at all!"

Isaac was sitting at the table; he stood up and said, "In honor of the fact that we just buried our dad, and to celebrate my last night in Hawaii, I think a little violence is in order."

Billy said, "What did you have in mind?"

Isaac responded, "PIG HUNT."

Michael said, "Isaac, we're Jews. We don't hunt pig."

Isaac said, "Michael, we're Jews. We don't *eat* pig."

Michael said, "I don't know if that's right, but it sounds good, and I'll go along with it."

The Grands were not *kosher*, per se. They ate shellfish, but they didn't really eat much pork. When the kids were in their early teens, the Grands once went to a Chinese restaurant and ordered *Mushu Chicken* instead of *Mushu Pork*. The waitress, who knew about five words of English, said, "*You no eat da pork—you da Jew?*" For weeks afterwards, Janice would ask Michael if he was *the* Jew. Michael would respond to Janice and say, "No, *you* are *the* Jew!" Janice would ask Isaac if he was *the* Jew, and Isaac would respond to Janice, "No, *you* are *the* Jew!" It got so annoying that Joshua would pull the car over every time they said it, turn the engine off, pull out a paperback book from his pocket, and start reading, greatly embarrassing his children.

Isaac, formulating a plan in his head, looked at Billy and said, "Billy, do you still know Sampson Chong?"

Billy said, "Yes, sir. I just saw him not long ago."

Isaac said to Billy, "Call him."

Michael said to Isaac, "Not my thing, Isaac. You guys go."

Isaac shot a look of disgust at Michael and told him, "No fucking way, brah—you're coming."

Michael said, "Diana wants to go out tonight."

Isaac said, "Mike, I am going back to Afghanistan in two days. I want you to come pig hunting with me and Billy."

Michael thought about it for a second, relented, and said, "Well, now that you say it like that, how can I refuse?"

Isaac said, "Billy, call Sampson."

"Will do. I will get some SWAT buddies to come, too. They'll get a kick out of meeting the Legend that is Isaac Grand."

While Isaac and Billy went off to find Sampson Chong and create their pig-hunt op, Michael was napping on the couch. He dreamed that his dad had come home, wearing his hospital gown. Joshua had all of his hair. Michael kept saying to his dad, "What are you doing here? I know that you died." Joshua was silent; he just stood there, smiling. Michael woke up suddenly, remembering the vivid dream, and hoped that he'd see his dad again in his dreams sometime.

Diana called. Michael told her that his plans had changed, that now he was going on a forced night march with his brother, and that it would probably go all night.

Diana asked if she could come.

"Diana, I don't know. With Billy and Isaac planning this thing, I bet there are going to be lots of firearms."

"Michael, when has that ever stopped me before? Do you not remember going hunting with your dad?"

Michael had actually repressed that memory. They had gone hunting on Lanai with Joshua exactly one week before he'd found Diana in bed with the other guy. It all came back to him. Michael said, "If you want to come with us tonight, I'm sure that Isaac will be fine with it, but he will make you carry your own shit and keep up."

"Um, excuse me, Michael. I'm in the Navy. I just did a GORUCK Tough. This will be the same thing, but more fun, and I can be armed."

"Fine—just don't shoot Isaac. Shoot Billy, but not Isaac."

"Deal."

"I think we're leaving the house at four. If you come over earlier, we can play doctor."

"Now you're talking."

"See you later."

"Bye. Love you."

Michael was a bit hesitant, and then he said it. "Love you."

Michael called Billy and told him that Diana was joining them. In the background, he could hear Isaac say, "Have her shoot Billy, not me." Michael snickered and hung up the phone.

Diana arrived at three. Everyone got to the house around three-thirty. Billy and Isaac showed up with a bag of greasy fast food. Isaac was eating a huge triple-decker burger.

Diana saw him chowing down, and said, "Isaac, when you clog your arteries and start having fucking chest pains and they send you to my clinic to give you a stress test and I can't clear you, you won't be able to go hang out with your MARSOC friends anymore."

Isaac grinned at her with an open mouthful of food, gave Diana a *shaka* sign, and said "Fucking A."

Diana giggled. Diana always liked to kid with Isaac about his incredibly awful diet, but she also knew that he had about 15% body fat and could bench press 350 pounds.

Michael overheard their conversation and said to them, "Wow! You two swear like sailors. Wait—you two *are* sailors."

CHAPTER 13

Billy walked in wearing tiger-stripe fatigues, a boonie hat, jungle boots, and a leather chest holster with his .45. He also had a machete strapped to his side. He gave a holstered .45 to Michael and said to him, "You remember how to use this?"

Michael said, "Yep."

Michael, Isaac, and Billy had grown up shooting and were very comfortable around firearms.

Billy gave a Beretta 92F to Diana. Diana said, "How come the girl gets the 9MM?"

Isaac laughed at her and said, "Because."

Billy walked out to his truck and came back with some fatigues, boots, and some rucksacks. Billy gave the fatigues and boots to Diana and said, "I have a buddy on SWAT who is about your size. These should fit."

Diana went off to change, and Billy gave out machetes and headlamps that were in one of his gear bags. Isaac checked all of the headlamps to see if their red filters worked and checked the sharpness on the machetes. He pulled out his Kimber Custom from his

GORUCK GR1 that had been all over the world with him, released the magazine, checked the slide action, looked down the barrel, reloaded the magazine, and put the handgun in a tactical side holster.

Michael knew better than to ask Isaac how he'd brought a loaded sidearm through airport security. Isaac put the GR1 on the table. Michael noticed that Isaac was in his own world. He was silent and methodical; he was preparing for an operation and didn't want to be bothered.

Diana came out and said, "I look like fucking Magnum P.I. Why do you SWAT guys wear tiger stripes?"

Billy replied, "Because they make you look like Magnum P.I. Women love us; guys want to be us." Billy walked to the kitchen and filled the hydration bladders with water. They loaded up and headed off to Sampson Chong's house in neighboring Kaneohe. Michael left a note for Sarah that read: "Dear mom, the clan + Diana went pig hunting. We will be home for dinner, and, no, we won't be eating pig."

Sampson Chong was a half-Hawaiian retired stevedore and Navy diver with a huge belly and a long grey beard who lived in a World War II Quonset hut up a long and deserted drive way off of Kaneohe Highway that most people didn't know existed. He had incredible views of Kaneohe Bay and was directly across from the Marine Base. Isaac had known Sampson for twenty-five years, Billy longer. The three of them would routinely hunt pigs. As Billy's truck drove up the long and winding overgrown highway, one of Sampson's dogs was barking at them, wary of the strangers. As soon as Billy rolled down his window and said, "Mokua, knock it off!" the dog quieted. Mokua turned around and ran to the Quonset hut, and Billy followed the dog slowly in his truck.

Sampson was standing in the doorway, talking with two other men. He was wearing olive drab fatigues and a "Divers Do It Deeper" t-shirt. Sampson's other dogs were barking in a fenced-in pen next to the house. Sampson screamed, "Hui, knock it off!" and the other dogs stopped barking. Isaac got out and hugged Sampson. Billy came over, and they hugged. Isaac hugged one of the men who was talking to Sampson. It was Noah Chong, Sampson's son, about the same age as Isaac. The other man was Sampson's friend Roland. Isaac hugged him, too. A few minutes later, Billy's friends showed up in their trucks. Sampson opened the fenced-in pen, and all six of his dogs ran out into the yard.

The *Pua* were initially brought to the islands by the original Polynesians, and the pigs quickly became feral. Later, Captain Cook introduced a different breed of pig that soon bred with the feral pig population and created a hardy survivor, growing to be a few hundred pounds. These wild boars were destructive to most native species of plants, birds, and some small animals, and hunting them was largely encouraged. The wild boars were also quite aggressive and had large, sharp tusks. By law, pig hunts could occur only one hour after sunset and one hour before sunrise. Sampson and Noah loaded the dogs into the back of Sampson's pickup truck, into a custom fenced-in cage anchored to the truck bed. Noah and Roland loaded up their gear, and everyone headed back to Kailua to the Norfolk area, where there were miles of trails that fed up to the mountains and to the Pali Highway above. It would be an ideal time to hunt pigs.

Sampson parked in a residential subdivision, and the two other pickup trucks parked behind him. There, Sampson let out the dogs, and they jumped down from the truck bed barking and wagging their tails in excited anticipation, as they knew what was coming. The group headed out, with the late-day sun sending long, low shadows through the Norfolk pines.

They walked for approximately a half-hour up the trail toward the mountains. Isaac was walking in front of Michael and said to his brother, "Hey, Mike—maybe we will see some *Night Marchers*."

Michael responded to his brother, "Don't you start."

Isaac laughed. Isaac knew that, as kids, his brother was terrified of the legend of the *Night Marchers*, the undead that would march for hours late at night. If someone saw them and didn't immediately bow and pay homage, they would steal their souls and force them to march with the group for all eternity. Everyone who lived in Hawaii would hear stories about seeing them walking, or hearing drums, or seeing lit torches that would suddenly disappear. Isaac swore he once saw *Night Marchers* one night when he was camping with his Boy Scout troop at Kaena Point. It was very late at night, and everyone else was asleep. Isaac first heard drums beating; then he saw two columns of walkers holding torches and walking into the sea. He watched in amazement as the torches slowly went below the waves. No one believed Isaac, but for years, he knew what he saw.

CHAPTER 14

The trails were muddy and slick; it started raining again, and soon everyone was soaked, their boots heavy with mud. The dogs started barking and ran off ahead. Isaac, Billy, and Sampson were right behind them. They walked up the trail toward the mountains for a mile. It was starting to get dark in the forest, and everyone switched on their headlamps, illuminating the trail ahead with white beams. The dogs soon caught a scent and started barking wildly. Two of the dogs suddenly ran off of the trail into a thicket of brush, and immediately, everyone heard squealing. They'd found a pig. The other dogs ran in and encircled the animal.

Isaac started sprinting and soon was right behind them and caught up to the dogs. Michael shone his headlamp in Isaac's direction and saw him draw his Kimber and pull out a Ka-Bar knife that was sheathed on his right side. Billy drew his .45. Sampson had an AR-15 on a tactical sling, and he brought it up to chest level. The pig was squealing, and the dogs were barking madly. Noah came running up, pistol in hand. Michael and Diana saw a dark movement in the brush ahead—they were just behind all of the action. The pig knew that it was cornered. Suddenly, it turned quickly and charged the dogs. Isaac was in the middle of the pack of dogs surrounding the pig. Michael saw a huge wild pig run right into one of the dogs, head down and low. One of the dogs let out a loud whimper. The pig then bounced right into Isaac. Isaac instantaneously pivoted and drove the Ka-Bar directly into the pig's spine below its head and fired two quick shots into its skull.

Michael had never seen anything so brutal and so elegant. The pig dropped like it had ran out of gas, all four legs splayed out. It let out what sounded like a sigh but was probably air escaping its lungs, and died. Isaac ran over to the dog. It was Mokua, the dog that had barked at Billy's truck when they drove up to meet Sampson. The pig had managed to get a tusk in right under the dog's rib cage and torn it open, to almost the dog's spine. Intestines and blood were pouring out of the large hole. The dog had labored, shallow breathing. Isaac knew it was dying. He immediately fired a round into the base of the dog's skull to end its suffering. The other dogs had stopped barking and had encircled Mokua.

Diana, Michael, and Sampson ran up to see Isaac standing over Mokua, the Kimber in hand. Isaac said, "I'm sorry about Mokua, Sampson. He was a brave dog."

Sampson responded, "Thank you for ending his suffering, brah."

It was then that Diana said, "Isaac, you're bleeding." In the darkness, the group all aimed their headlights at Isaac and could see that Isaac's right pant leg was covered in blood below the knee. Isaac found a hole in his pants and tore it open to see an angry six-inch gash on his shin below his knee. He was able to see bone. Isaac sat down. Diana ran over.

Isaac said, "It is not pumping. That's a good sign."

But blood was pouring out. Diana put her hand over the injury.

Isaac said, "Michael, can you get into my pack and pull out my blow-out bag?"

The GR1 was still on Isaac's back. Michael reached in and found a small pouch with a Red Cross patch on it and gave it to Isaac. Isaac opened the khaki-colored pouch, grabbed the packet of combat gauze, which contained a quick-clotting agent, tore it open, and stuffed the contents into his wound. Isaac held his hands over the wound tightly for five minutes. He found the Israeli-made trauma-wound dressing, tore open the package, and wrapped it tightly around his shin. He opened another package of military-issue olive drab bandage and wrapped it over the trauma dressing.

Isaac turned to Diana and said, "Hey, doc. I think you're going to have to patch me up."

Sampson and Noah cut down a small tree. They stripped the branches and had the pig tied up, ready for transport, together, they would carry it out.

Billy grabbed Mokua's body, swung it up over his big shoulders, and carried it out. Diana asked Isaac if he could walk, and Isaac nodded. Diana and Michael walked carefully with Isaac to make sure that he wouldn't slip on the muddy trail. What took 30 minutes of walking into the trail took two and a half hours walking out.

By the time they got to the trucks, the neighborhood was pitch black, but the trucks were illuminated by one lone street lamp that lit up the neighborhood cul-de-sac. Sampson, Noah, Billy, Michael, and Diana all lifted the pig up and threw it on the hood of Sampson's truck, and Sampson and Noah tied it down. Sampson said that they would have normally gutted and dressed the pig on the trail, but because of Isaac's injury, they would do that later, at Sampson's house. By 10 PM, they would have the pig gutted, dressed, covered in banana leaves, and put in the *Imu* for at least 12 hours of slow, underground cooking on lava rocks. Sampson said that they were all invited over tomorrow to help eat the pig, *Luau* style. Isaac and Michael both laughed. Diana, Isaac, and Michael all crammed into Billy's truck. Isaac was lying in the truck bed, his leg propped up on the various rucks.

By the time Billy pulled into the driveway, Sarah and Janice had returned from Waikiki. Diana went out to her car and got her trauma bag; it was fully equipped to handle most medical emergencies. She always had it in the car, as she often made the drive to Tripler from Kailua over an isolated two-lane dark highway that was poorly lit; drunk soldiers would routinely wreck their cars. Sarah saw Isaac limping in, soaked, muddy, and bloody.

Billy was right behind him and said, "Mrs. Grand, I know that you are going to yell at me for tracking mud into your house, but this is an emergency."

Janice came out and saw Isaac. She turned to her brother and said, "Michael, get all that stuff off of the dining room table." Michael cleared the table.

Janice, continuing, said, "Isaac, go lie on the table."

Michael said, "Wait—don't you think he should go to the Emergency Room?"

Janice said, "Why, we have a perfectly staffed medical unit right here." Janice was an orthopedic surgeon who took trauma call. Diana was a hospitalist and an internist. Sarah had been an ER nurse for her whole career—it was where she'd first met Joshua. Joshua was on leave from Vietnam, and he borrowed a buddy's 1964 Yamaha motorcycle and went off to ride around the island. He wrecked it going around a corner too fast and rode it to Queen's Medical Center because he thought that, if he went to Tripler, they would throw him in the brig for destruction of military property. Sarah was the one who'd cleaned and bandaged him up. It was love at first sight, but Joshua didn't want to get involved with Sarah, because if he were to be killed in combat in Vietnam, he knew that it might break Sarah's heart. Sarah insisted, and they had what amounted to a whirlwind romance before Joshua got on the transport plane back to Vietnam.

Diana came in with the trauma kit, reached in for a packet of latex gloves, and gave a pair to both Sarah and Janice. Sarah took off Isaac's boots while Diana cut away his pants. Diana noticed Isaac's penis and said, "Damn, Isaac. What do they feed you in Afghanistan? That thing is huge! Michael, if you ever get tired of me, I'm going to call your brother!"

Isaac said, "Don't make me laugh."

Janice shook her head and giggled. She cut off the dressing that Isaac had applied on the trail; it was saturated with blood. Janice felt Isaac's foot; it was neither hot nor cold to the touch. Janice asked Isaac to wiggle his toes; he did. She poked the bottom of Isaac's foot with the tip of the surgical shears that were in her hand and asked him if he could feel what she was doing. Isaac nodded. Isaac told Janice the wound was throbbing.

Janice pulled out the quick-clot gauze that Isaac had shoved into the wound, and Janice noted that there was minimal bleeding. Diana reached over with a bottle of saline and cleaned out the wound. Sarah covered the site with Betadine. Diana took out a syringe and told

Isaac that she was going to numb the area with some Lidocaine. Isaac could feel the needle going in; then, a few seconds later, he said that he was starting to feel the Lido working. Janice opened the wound and looked in but said that she needed more light. Michael took off his headlamp, adjusted it, turned it on, and put it on Janice's head. Janice looked into Isaac's leg and said, while probing around in Isaac's leg, "The fibula looks good. There are no fractures. Looks like that pig missed all vital areas." Janice kept probing and said, "The pig sliced one of your muscles pretty deeply, but I can fix that. I can numb it, but it's going to hurt like hell when the needle goes in. Isaac, you're going to be sore for a while, but I think that you're going to live."

Isaac grimaced and clenched his fists against the dining-room table as Janice injected the Lidocaine directly into his muscle. Diana gave Janice a suture pack, and Janice sewed up the muscle while Diana held open the wound. Sarah cleaned the wound out again with saline, and Janice debrided the wound and then stitched it closed.

Diana gave Isaac a shot of antibiotics and said, "Isaac, I am going to put you on Keflex. Pigs are disgusting animals, and I don't want that wound to get infected. I am also going to get you some pain medications. I'll run over to the clinic at Kaneohe and grab those. I suspect that the Lido will be wearing off pretty soon."

Sarah started to wrap the wound with clean gauze and re-wrapped it with some olive drab combat bandages that were in Diana's bag.

Diana said, "Hey, Isaac. If you don't want to go back to Afghanistan, I can give you a doctor's note." Isaac said that wasn't an option. Diana knew this but liked to poke fun at Isaac whenever she had the chance. Diana took off the gloves and said that she was going out, that she would be back in about an hour.

"Michael, do you want to come with me?"

"Sure, but let me grab a change of clothes. I'm soaked, and I smell. Hey, guys—we'll pick up some Chinese food for dinner." Isaac chimed in while still lying on the kitchen table and told them to get some beer.

CHAPTER 15

Michael and Diana stopped at Diana's house so that they could clean up. They showered together in silence, kissed, and let the steam envelop them in Diana's little shower. Diana said that she missed this, and Michael agreed. They went to the clinic on the base so that Diana could get Isaac's medications, and they called in an order to the little Chinese restaurant in Kailua. On the drive back to the house, in the dark car, Michael said, "I'm in love with you. I always have been, but are you going to break my heart again? Because there is only so much I can take at this point in my life. If this is just a fling because you're lonely, just let me go back to Atlanta and wallow in my misery."

Diana, driving, grabbed Michael's left hand and said, "Michael, you're not a consolation prize. You're a blue ribbon. I didn't really understand that until you left. I am at a better place in my life than I was back then."

Michael, slowly nodding his head, said, "How do I know that you won't cheat on me again?"

Diana started crying and said, "Michael, that was the single worst thing I've ever done to anyone, including myself. I have gone over it again and again in my mind, and I don't really want to go back there. I love you, too, and I wouldn't do anything to jeopardize that."

Michael said, "Promise?"

"Promise. I love you."

Michael smiled as he said, "I love you, too."

Sarah and Janice had cleaned and scrubbed the table after Michael and Diana had left. Isaac had found the remaining Hinano beer in the fridge and proceeded to self-medicate out on the rear Lanai. The rain had stopped, and Isaac listened to the sound of the surf coming in and rolling up over the sand. Michael and Diana returned, and they all ate cashew chicken, Singapore noodles, walnut shrimp, Mushu Chicken, and seafood bird's nest, and drank Kirin Ichiban on the kitchen table that, two hours before, had been an operating table.

Michael grabbed a couple of quilts from the house and some of the remaining beer and went down to the beach. He spread out the quilts and sat cross-legged, staring at the sky. As a boy, he would love to come down to the beach and count how many satellites he could see moving in the sky. He was up to twenty when Diana and Isaac joined him. He handed a beer to both. Michael asked his brother how he was feeling.

Isaac said, "Hurts like a fucker, but the beer helps." The pain meds had not kicked in yet, but Isaac had a nice little beer buzz going on.

They talked about the pig hunt, Joshua, and how nice the night had turned out, despite what had happened earlier.

Michael asked his brother about Afghanistan. He knew that certainly operational issues were off limits and that, frankly, his brother would never tell him anything.

"How's it going over there? Every time I hear about some service member getting killed 'while on combat operations,' my heart always stops for a second, and I hope that I don't find out it's you."

Isaac said, "Michael, it is my great honor to serve my country there and to be able to lead some incredible men."

Michael said, "Do you ever get tired of it?"

Diana chimed in and said, "Michael, serving is one of the great responsibilities that we do selflessly. It has been a great privilege for me to serve my country."

Isaac said, "Do I get tired of it? Sometimes. The Navy sucks balls, and they make can make life not fun, but I am doing something that I truly love to do, and I work with some amazing people."

Michael said, "Judging by how you killed that pig today, you're probably pretty good at it, too."

Isaac responded, "Michael, I take no pride in removing bad men from the battlefield who are trying to kill me and my friends or who try to threaten our way of life."

Michael said to his brother, "I get that, but, man—that was art."

Isaac said nothing.

At that moment, Michael realized that, despite all of the deployments, the combat, the trauma, the terror, the boredom, and everything else that goes on, more than fifteen years of war had not destroyed Isaac's humanity.

They all talked for a bit longer, and the three silently watched the sky together. Isaac said that he was pretty buzzed and that he was going to sleep. He stumbled back up the beach to the house.

Diana and Michael covered up with one of the quilts and watched the moonlight reflect off the ocean. They made out for a little bit, and then lay together in each other's arms.

Diana said, "Can I sleep over tonight?"

Michael responded, stroking Diana's hair, "Remember, I have that little full-size bed in my room."

Diana giggled and said, "It hasn't stopped us in the past."

Michael thought about that for a second and said, "True." Michael and Diana went back to the house. Everyone was asleep, but Sarah had left the living-room lights on for them. Diana went into Michael's bedroom while Michael turned off the lights. They both immediately fell asleep.

Diana woke up at sunrise, got up, and tried to not wake Michael, who was sleeping peacefully. Diana found Michael's t-shirt on the floor, put it on, and went out into the kitchen to make some coffee. She found Sarah in the kitchen, making banana bread. Sarah saw Diana and said, "Good morning, love."

Diana said, "Good morning. How did you sleep?"

Sarah responded, "Well, I think I was worn out from an eventful day yesterday."

Diana grabbed a mug of coffee from Sarah's outstretched hand and said, "I'm sure."

Sarah said, "Thanks for your help with Isaac last night; this isn't the first time that we have patched him up in the kitchen. He was always getting into trouble when he was a kid."

Diana responded, "Happy to help."

Sarah turned to Diana and said, "It's nice to see that you're back in the family again. I hope you stick around for a while. I just wish

Joshua were here to see that you and Michael are back together. He always liked you."

Diana started to tear up and said to Sarah, "I like being around. You have a great family."

Janice and Isaac were both leaving later in the day. Sarah had washed all of Isaac's clothes.

CHAPTER 16

Janice went to go walk the beach for one more time. When she got back, she went to sit on the couch next to Sarah who was reading a book. "Mom, I was thinking. Thanksgiving is in two weeks. It was always Dad's favorite holiday. I know that we really don't have much to be thankful for, but how would you feel about hosting the whole family here? Dan might not be able to get time off, but the kids would be thrilled to *come out to Hawaii to spend time with Grandma.*"

Sarah put her book down. "Honey, I don't know. It's a lot of work, and I don't have much energy to be entertaining."

Janice thought for a minute and said, "I'll do it. I'll do all of the cooking."

Michael chimed in, "I'll help. My trial should be done by then. I'll come back."

Sarah was a wonderful cook, but Michael and Janice were equally good in their own right, and both loved to cook.

Diana said, "Hey, I can buy the pies and the wine!"

Sarah said, "Okay. If you guys can come out, we can host Thanksgiving here."

There was a collective cheer. "*Ssh*. You will wake up your brother."

Diana said, "Isaac was probably pretty stoned on codeine and beer last night. I think a bomb going off in the kitchen wouldn't wake him up."

Diana went home to shower and get ready for work, but Sarah invited her over for dinner later, and she said that she would be there.

Michael decided to walk the beach. He changed into surf trunks, took his iPod, put on sunscreen, and headed out. Michael was thinking about the events of the past few days. He'd lost his dad, his rock, but he'd found Diana. He was here with his entire family, which made him happy. Billy was here, too. *I'm sure there's a lesson somewhere in there*, he thought to himself. From the beach, Michael saw the dark shapes of turtles swimming below the surface. Their heads would occasionally pop to the surface and look around. Michael remembered that, as kids, long before there was any federal law protecting the Green Sea Turtle, he and Isaac used to ride them. They would swim up to them underwater and grab on to the shell right above their flippers, careful not to touch their beaks, which would take a finger off like it was nothing. They could ride the turtles for miles out to sea; if they weren't paying attention, they would have to make the long swim back. Isaac always thought that the turtle was his *amakua*, his protective spirit, and whenever he went into a combat zone, he always took a small carved sea turtle with him.

Michael decided to jump into the ocean. He took off his shirt, put his flip-flops and iPod in the middle, and placed the pile on the sand. He dove in, the water initially shocking him; then he got used to it. Michael was a strong swimmer. He did a quick breast stroke for about 1000 yards, and then he turned over onto his back and floated, staring at the clouds forming above. When Michael came back, he used the outside shower to wash the sand off his feet.

He walked in and saw Isaac in the kitchen staring at the open fridge, looking for something to eat. Sarah had gone off to the grocery store to get some food. Isaac was the only guy he knew who could survive a brush with a wild boar only to wake up the next day starving.

"Man, you slept like twelve hours. How do you feel?"

Isaac said, "A little sore. I'll go for a swim later; the saltwater will help heal the wound."

Michael sat down next to Isaac and said, "You are going to have a bad-ass scar there; chicks will dig it. After you eat breakfast, come with me. I want to show you some things that dad wanted you to have." They finished the last bit of *chow fun* from the memorial gathering.

Michael got up from the table and put his dishes in the sink. Isaac did the same. Michael told his brother to follow him, and he went out to the garage. The garage was mostly a shrine to all things from Michael and Isaac's past adventures and hobbies. The mountain bikes, windsurfer sails, scuba tanks, climbing gear, tents, sleeping bags, reloading station, and remnants of a darkroom were all still there. Over the years, Sarah had threatened to give it all away because it was taking up space in the small garage, but in the end, she could never bear to part with all of the boys' things. Michael pointed to where the Harley was covered under an old blanket and said to Isaac, "Brother, that's for you. Dad wanted you to have it."

Isaac knew exactly what it was. He had ridden his dad's bike hundreds of times. "Are you *fucking kidding me*?!"

"No, sir. It's yours."

"Man, dad loved that bike," Isaac said and just stood there, staring at the Harley.

Michael continued, "Um, actually, he loved that *you loved* that bike. I saw him ride it only a few times."

Isaac walked over to where the bike was, pulled the blanket off, and got on. He put his hands on the handlebar grips and removed them to rub the gas tank. He said, "I learned how to ride on this bike."

Michael said, "Me, too."

Isaac continued, "Man, I'll think of dad every single time I ride it," as he started to choke up. He continued, "I am going to strip it down to the frame and rebuild it. I think I'll powder-coat the frame and paint the tank and fenders matte black. It'll look cool with a nice California-style handlebar on it." He placed his hand on the side shifter.

Michael looked at his brother and said, "Okay, you just told the universe that you'll come back alive from Afghanistan. You'll be cursed if you renege on that promise."

"Mike, I have every intention of coming back alive from Afghanistan. I've lost too many friends in that place, and that will not happen to me."

"Promise?"

"Brah, I promise from the bottom of my heart," Isaac said. He got off of the Harley, and he and Michael embraced.

Michael walked toward the open garage door and told his brother, "Alright, Hanukkah is coming early this year. There are more goodies—come with me." Michael went into the house, into their dad's study. He walked to his dad's desk and opened the drawer where he knew that his dad kept the key to the antique armoire that held the guns. Michael opened the glass double doors to where the shotguns were held. There were various shotguns in the case. There was a Purdey & Sons, a Holland & Holland Royal Hammerless side by side, a Parker V, a Beretta 687, and an Orvis Uplander.

Michael told his brother, "Dad wanted us to split them up. You first. Take your pick."

"Isaac said, "The Purdey gives me a chub, and so does the Holland & Holland." He reached in, grabbed the Holland & Holland, hefted it, and eyed it over. Holding the shotgun, he said, "Man, I forgot how beautiful this fucker is. Can I have those two?" Both brothers knew that, combined, the two guns were worth more than $20,000.

Michael proudly said, "They're yours. I'll take the Parker V and the Beretta. I will give the Orvis Uplander to Diana. It's a 20-gauge."

Isaac giggled. "Brah, what is up with you and Diana? Are you back together for good this time?"

"Brother, I haven't told anyone this yet, but I'm going to ask her to marry me. I want you to be my best man. We'll do it when you come back from deployment."

Isaac said he'd be honored and hugged his brother.

Sarah came home and fixed a salad for lunch. They all sat around the kitchen table, talking. "How great is it for me to have all my babies in one place!"

Janice said, "We love being here, mom."

CHAPTER 17

The rain started again, and Michael opened up the sliding doors to hear the sound of the rain. Isaac finished lunch, took a nap, borrowed a pair of his brother's swim trunks, and went off to soak in the ocean. Michael decided to go with his brother and figured that he was already going to get wet from the rain. The two began to horseplay in the water like they were kids again. For the first time in a long time, Michael felt like he didn't have the weight of the world on his shoulders and that Atlanta, with all of its associated stress, was a million miles away, and that maybe he should think about moving back home.

Sarah was napping on the couch, and Janice had taken her mom's car into Kailua town to mail some postcards to the kids. Isaac went in to pack his gear and get ready for his long flight back to the war. Michael texted Diana and sent her heart emoticons like a lusty thirteen-year-old. She texted hearts back. Michael fell asleep with a smile on his face and awoke as the sun was setting through his bedroom window.

Diana called Sarah and told her that she would take care of dinner. Later, Diana came over with two huge trays of sushi and a case of Kirin Ichiban.

Isaac said, "Diana, that was very thoughtful of you to bring me all that beer."

Before they ate, they held hands, and Sarah thanked them all for coming out to help celebrate the life of Joshua Grand. "I could not have gone through this without all of your support. Thank you."

They ate their sushi and drank their Kirin, listening to some of Joshua's favorite music, including Jefferson Airplane, the Beatles, the Rolling Stones, Creedence Clearwater Revival, and when Dick Dale's *Hava Nagila* came on, they up got up and danced a *hora* in Joshua's memory. Diana and Michael took Isaac and Janice to separate airports. Michael, driving Diana's old Lexus LS 400, took Janice to the United Airlines terminal at Honolulu International Airport and Isaac to Hickam so that Isaac could board a C-17 for the 15-hour flight to Bagram. At the departures area at HNL, they all got out of the car and hugged. Isaac thanked Janice and Diana for sewing him up. Janice gave him her extra Ambien, saying that he would need them more than her, but Diana told him to take only 10MGs even though she knew that he would take double that amount.

Michael looked at the bottle of Ambien and said, out loud to no one in particular, "I don't know what y'all see in that stuff. I took one of those once, and I don't know if I hallucinated or dreamt, but I woke up to a bear trying to violate me."

Diana looked at him, rolled her eyes, and said, "How old are you?"

Michael gave her a big open-mouth grin in response.

Michael watched Janice make her way into the agricultural inspection line and drove off to Hickam, which was just down the road. At Hickam, Michael, Isaac, and Diana all hugged.

"Stay safe over there."

"Thank you, brother. I will."

Diana gave him a double-strand *pikake* lei that she'd picked up at a lei shop in Chinatown on the way home. They hugged. Isaac told them both he would see them soon. Michael watched his brother enter the terminal, and he drove off. Diana wanted to go to the Hickam Officers Club, which was right next to the runway, to watch Isaac's plane take off. Diana ordered a red wine, and Michael ordered a scotch, neat. They waited a few minutes as other airplane traffic taxied up and took off. When Isaac's C-17 taxied over the takeoff point and then spun up its engines and roared down the runway, they raised their drinks in tribute to Isaac. Michael watched as the big transport plane took off and became smaller and smaller, finally disappearing over the horizon.

"I sure hope he comes back," Michael said.

"He will."

Diana wanted Michael to spend the night at her house because her bed was bigger, but Michael said that he didn't want his mom to be alone but that she was welcome to spend another night with him on his childhood bed. Diana told him that she loved sleeping next to him but that she needed to get some sleep on a bigger bed. She said that she was working at Kaneohe tomorrow and could stop by for lunch.

"I'll take you to Buzz's."

"Deal."

She dropped Michael off; they kissed for a while in the driveway, and Michael told her to sleep well, that he would talk to her tomorrow. Diana drove off with a smile on her face. Michael fell asleep almost instantaneously. He woke up to the sunrise, and Sarah was already up.

Sarah asked her son, "Want to walk the beach? We can go to *Kalapawai* and get some Kona coffee and walk back."

Michael said, "Love to."

Michael and Sarah walked the length of the beach and back, holding hands and talking about Joshua. They finished their walk and got coffee from the *Kalapawai* market. They were walking back down the beach toward the house, and Michael said, "I am going to ask Diana to marry me. Do you think that I can call Harry?"

His mom started crying. Harry Goldberg was the family jeweler. He was Moshe's friend and was older than dirt. He'd gone to Joshua and Sarah's wedding, and all of the kids' Bar and Bat Mitzvahs. "Harry would be honored. You have made an old woman's heart very happy."

Michael checked his email, texted with Diana, texted with Janice, who was back in Denver, and called Harry. Harry told him to come down around three. Michael's phone rang. He recognized the number—it was his old boss, Marvin Wong. Marvin was the senior managing partner at Wong, Miller, Abernathy, and Konishige, one of Hawaii's best law firms, and he was the president of the Hawaii Trial Lawyers Association.

Michael answered his phone, and Marvin said, "Hey, *boychik*, what's new?"

Marvin was a longtime friend of Michael's dad. Joshua had set Marvin up with his wife. Marvin was a member of Joshua's monthly poker game, and Joshua had gotten Michael the job at Marvin's firm when he finished his first year in law school, and Michael was Marvin's summer law clerk. When Michael graduated from law school, he was hired on as an associate. Marvin was always known as "Uncle

Marvin" to Michael, as everyone in Hawaii has many non-relative *calabash* "Aunties" and "Uncles."

Over time, Marvin had become a mentor to Michael, a relationship that Michael truly loved. Michael had worked at WMAK for ten years before he moved to Atlanta because of a girl. Over time, Marvin had grown to love Michael like another son.

"I didn't get to your dad's funeral. I was doing a depo in San Francisco, but you and your family have been in my thoughts."

"Thank you for the beautiful flowers, Marvin." Even though Jews largely don't believe in flowers at funerals, the big, gregarious Chinese senior partner did and sent the family a very expensive arrangement of tropical flowers.

"You're welcome."

Michael was happy to hear from his old boss and said, "I actually wanted to call you. I'm thinking, mulling over, coming back. I am tired of the grind in Atlanta. I was wondering if there was still any place for me at the firm."

Marvin replied, "Michael, you are welcome back at any time, but I think I might have a better offer. Can we meet for lunch early next week?"

Michael responded, "Marvin, aside from being at the airport at 10 PM on Thursday, I have nowhere else to be."

Marvin said, "Great. Let's do Tuesday. Swing by the office around 11:30 and say hello. I bet there are a few people around who will want to see you."

"Will do, Marvin. Thank you."

CHAPTER 18

Michael showered, got dressed, and took the 280SL out for the quick trip to Buzz's. The sun had come out for the first time in days, so Michael put the top down. Buzz's Original Steak House was one of the last reminders of when Hawaii was a gentler place. Literally a grass shack, the restaurant had been around since the early 1960s. They took cash only, had Hinano on tap, and they always broadcast what fresh fish was on the menu by raising the equivalent fish flag on their flagpole. The fish flags were prevalent on the piers where fishing boats moored. The captains would fly the flags, letting everyone know what was in the hold. Buzz's salad bar was also world famous. Movie stars, ex-presidents, and locals alike all loved the place.

Diana was waiting for him on a bench outside when he showed up. She was wearing her tan Navy uniform, as she'd come from work. They kissed. Diana looked at Michael getting out of the 280SL and said, "That car becomes you."

Michael said, "I love that car."

They sat at a table facing a beach park and the ocean across the street. They watched one of the local canoe clubs get ready for an afternoon paddle. The server thanked Diana for her service. They held hands across the table.

Michael looked at Diana and asked her how her day was going, so far.

Diana responded, "Not bad. The clinic is light today. Nothing serious."

Michael continued, "My old boss called me today. He said he wanted to talk to me about something."

Diana, between bites of her salad, said, "Really? That's great! Does that mean that maybe you would move back?"

Michael said, "I'm thinking about it. I'm tired of Atlanta."

Diana spent the rest of the lunch beaming. They split a homemade mud pie for dessert, and Michael paid the bill. They held hands walking out to their cars. Michael kissed Diana and said, "I have to go into town on a secret mission, but I will be back around six. What time are you working until?"

Diana, curious, said, "Hmm...what kind of secret mission?"

Michael responded playfully, "I can't tell you—it's a secret."

"Tell me, Michael!"

Michael continued the charade. "No. But I want to see you later. Can I come by?"

"Sure!"

"I'll probably take my mom to dinner, get her out of the house. You can come if you want."

Diana thought about it a minute and said, "I might be interested. I have laundry to do. I'll let you know."

"Okay. Love you."

"Love you."

They kissed and left in separate directions. Diana went back to work at the marine base, and Michael drove into Honolulu.

Michael took the 280SL up the winding road of the Pali. Dave Brubeck's *Take Five* was playing on the original Becker radio, one of his favorite songs. Michael opened it up. The 280SL was originally designed for drivers who complained that the 190SL didn't have enough power. The 280SL, for its time, was one of the best driving cars. Michael downshifted coming into turns and sped up coming out of them. It was a nice moment.

Michael parked in Harry's building, and his assistant buzzed him in when he got to the front door. Alexandra had been Harry's assistant for more than 30 years, and she'd watched Michael grow up. They hugged.

Alexandra said, "I am so sorry about your dad. He was a great man."

"Thanks. I miss him."

"So, Harry tells me that you need a ring. It's about time, Michael Grand! We're thrilled!"

Harry came out. He looked older than when Michael had last seen him, but he was still spry.

"Michael, *Mazel Tov!*" They hugged. Harry said, "My condolences about your dad. Alexandra took me to the funeral, but I didn't want to stay. At my age, there are only so many funerals I can sit through.

"Thank you for your kind words, Harry, and thank you for your well wishes. I think that this one is a keeper. I want to get her something nice."

Harry said, "We'll take good care of you. It's going to give me great pleasure to help you, and I'm so glad that you came here. Let's look at some stones."

Michael and Harry spent the next two hours going through loose diamonds. In the end, they both decided that a nice 2.5 carat stone had the nicest cut, color, and clarity. Harry set it in a simple white-gold prong setting. Harry had Alexandra model it, and she said, "Wow, that is some stone. Michael, if she says 'No,' I'll marry you!"

Michael put the ring on his Amex, and Harry put it in a nice red presentation box. "She's going to be thrilled, young man. *Mazel Tov* again!" They shook hands, and Michael left.

Michael drove the long way home, down past the Ala Wai Canal with the big palm trees. Joshua used to tell Michael that the reason there were palm trees between the road and the canal was because, when Joshua a teenager, he and his friends would water ski behind cars, and the local neighbors would complain. Michael drove the 280SL up past Kahala, past Hawaii Kai, Sandy Beach, where he and Isaac used to body surf as kids, past the beach that was made famous where Burt Lancaster kissed Debra Kerr in the surf in *From Here to Eternity*, past the Makapuu light house. He pulled into the scenic lookout and watched a pair of whales breach off of Rabbit Island. Michael was truly at peace.

He drove through Waimanalo and eventually turned right on the road that would take him home to Kailua.

It was late afternoon when he arrived home. Sarah was sitting in her favorite chair, staring out at the ocean.

"Hi, Honey. I didn't hear you come in. I must have been lost in my thoughts."

Michael said, "Harry sends his regards. He said he went to the funeral but didn't stay."

Sarah responded, "I saw him. He said some nice words to me before the services started."

"I didn't see him. Where was I?"

"You were off in another world, Michael."

Michael thought about what his mom had just said. "Probably true. There's not much I remember about that day."

"That's part of the grieving process, Dear Heart. Just know that Isaac, Janice, and I are all going through this in our own way. Michael, grief doesn't travel in a normal path. You can be good one day and overcome by pain and sorrow the next. We all have to take this one day at a time."

Sitting down on the couch next to Sarah's chair, Michael said, "I miss him, mom. I think about him every day."

"We all do, Honey—even Janice. Janice told me that she and Dan are going to divorce."

Michael was a little stunned but not surprised. "Was this because of dad?"

Sarah looked at her hands resting in her lap and replied, "Not really. Janice has been unhappy for a while, but your dad's death brought this decision into focus; she thinks life is too short to be unhappy with someone. She said she always wanted what Dad and I had. It breaks my heart, but I understand, and we'll all get by."

"Wow. She didn't tell me this."

"Michael, this is why I told you to forgive Diana. You're 45 years old; you don't need to spend the rest of your life alone."

"Speaking of which, check this out." Michael pulled out the ring box and handed it to his mom.

Sarah's heart raced as she opened the box. "Oh, my boy! Oh. I don't know what to say. This ring is beautiful. I am so thrilled!" She looked at her son and saw some hesitation in his face.

"Michael, what's wrong?"

"Nothing."

"Michael David Grand, I have known you your entire life. I have always known when you lie to me. What's wrong?"

Michael was about to speak.

His mom asked him, "Are you not 100% set on Diana?"

Michael responded, slowly, "No, mom. It isn't that. Diana is one of the best things that ever happened to me. It just took me a long time and several million brain cells to figure that out. No, I am going to ask Diana Eisenberg to marry me, and I hope she says 'Yes,' because I want to spend the rest of my life with her. I am worried that the other shoe is going to drop. I have had nice things happen lately, and I'm worried that something bad is going to happen that takes this all away."

Sarah looked at her son and said, "Michael, you were a philosophy major at BU. You know the universe doesn't work that way. Bad things don't happen in twos or threes or however else the myth goes."

Michael interrupted his mom. "But Isaac getting injured and Janice's divorce are related."

Michael's thought trailed off, and his mom said, "Michael, let me finish. These things are not related. Janice was going to do this months ago, but she dutifully stuck it out in therapy because of the kids. And your brother? *Hashem* knows that he has always found danger. Remember when he jumped off the roof, or when he bit the neighbor's dog, and the dog bit him back, and he came into the kitchen in a bloody mess? The other night was not the first time that I had to clean him up in the kitchen. These bad things were not related to your dad's death. We've all had enough bad luck lately and are all due for a little happiness—you included. It took you to bury your dad to figure out that there are things in your life that you wanted to make better, Diana is a keeper, and you deserve to be happy. I'm so thrilled for you!"

Sarah's words sunk in, and for the second time that day, Michael felt at peace.

CHAPTER 19

Diana decided to join Michael and Sarah out at dinner. They went to a neighborhood Italian place that Joshua loved. Michael ordered the chicken Marsala in honor of his dad. It was his favorite dish there, and he always ordered it, even when there was something exotic sounding on the specials board. Diana ordered eggplant parmesan, and Sarah ordered a piece of salmon, well done. They all ordered wine, and they talked.

Diana kept looking at Sarah and thought to herself that she looked contemplative. Maybe she was in the accepting phase of Joshua's death. Sarah ordered pistachio ice cream and tiramisu for the table. Michael paid the bill, and they drove Sarah home. After they talked for a while, Sarah kissed Diana and Michael goodnight and went to bed. Michael got three quilts out of the linen closet, kicked his shoes off, and headed down to the beach. Diana followed him, her shoes in her right hand. Michael laid out two of the quilts, and he and Diana lay down and stared at the stars. They started kissing.

"Thank you for entertaining my mom tonight. It means a lot to her that you're back in her life."

"Your mom is a great lady. It was the least that I could do," said Diana.

Michael propped himself up on one elbow and was rubbing Diana's hand. "You are one of the best things that ever happened to me. I am glad you broke up with that fucking *putz*."

"Well, thank you, counselor."

"You're welcome, doctor."

"I'm kind of glad he didn't work out, too. I kind of like you."

Michael reached over and covered them with one of the quilts, and they made love on the beach under the moonlight, listening to the waves crash in. Diana went home. Michael walked to the house and climbed into bed. For the second night in a row, Michael fell asleep immediately.

Michael woke, and Sarah was in the kitchen. Michael looked at the clock on the wall—it was almost 10 AM. "Holy shit! I slept late!"

Sarah said, "I figured you were tired, and I didn't want to wake you. There is some coffee and fresh strawberry papaya on the counter."

Michael loved strawberry papaya and ate the pinkish orange flesh down to the skin and savored his coffee. Michael and Sarah sat at the kitchen table.

"When are you going to propose?"

"I have to figure that out. I want to wait for the right time."

"Your father proposed to me in Moshe's shop. It was perfect."

"I need to find my equivalent of Moshe's shop. Let me think about this."

Sarah asked her son, "When do you meet with Marvin?"

"Tomorrow at 11:30."

"That will be nice. Marvin is a true *mensch*, and he's been very good to you over the years."

"Mom, I'm not happy in Atlanta, and I'm really burnt out in my job. If Marvin offered me a job, I would be inclined to take it. I pay a crazy amount of rent for my place in Buckhead, and I could wind down my practice pretty quickly. I don't care if I'm on the partner track there. I can't do what I am doing anymore. I've felt more human in the past few days than I have in the past few years. I am still barred here—I can make it work. Hawaii is my home. I can make it work."

Sarah started crying. "Michael, your father tried to get you back here for the past six years. But you're stubborn, just like him, and he knew that you would not want to come back, because he was worried that you would always have a big pair of shoes to fill by being Joshua Grand's son. But, he always knew that you could do it. He had such great faith in you. I am just sorry to know that he wasn't around to see you return."

Michael looked into his empty coffee cup and said, "Well, first things first. I have to see if I can get my old job back."

Michael texted Diana and asked how her day was, that he was thinking of her. She replied a few minutes later that she was pretty busy but that she was thinking of him, too. He asked if she wanted to grab dinner later, and she responded that she would love to but that maybe they could cook together instead of going out. Michael responded by asking Diana if aliens had replaced his girlfriend with a clone, that she hated to cook. She replied that it would be nice to spend time together doing something creative. Michael loved the idea and told her that they would talk later.

He texted Billy and asked him to meet him for lunch at Maui Taco. Billy said he was in court in Honolulu but would be done at noon and that he would be there at twelve-thirty.

The sun was out. Michael grabbed his iPod and took a quick walk down the beach. He saw lots of people walking and stopped to pet all the dogs that were friendly, especially those who were playing in the surf. *Dogs love the surf*, Michael thought. He came home and showered and changed into cargo shorts, a t-shirt, and black flip-flops.

When Michael arrived at Maui Taco, Billy was writing a ticket for someone who was parked in a handicapped parking spot without a handicapped window card. Michael saw what his friend was doing and said, "I hate that."

"Me, too," said Billy. They fist-bumped.

As they ate *Ahi* burritos, Michael showed Billy the ring. Billy said loudly, "Fuck, brah! That's a big stone! Are you proposing to me! Yes, Michael! I say 'Yes'!" A few other patrons turned around to see what was going on, but as soon as they saw a large man in an HPD uniform, they lost interest.

Michael said to his friend, "Not you, asshole, and, besides, Kimberly would kill me."

Billy laughed.

Billy asked Michael when he was going to propose.

Michael told him he was waiting for the right time.

Billy said, "Remember, I proposed to Kimberly up at your folks' cabin up in Kokee. You should take her up there."

"I don't know if we have time, Bill. I leave in a few days."

"Maybe I can fake-arrest her and take her to your mom's house. You and your mom can make a road of rose petals leading into the house, light some candles. Kimberly always says that candles put her in the mood."

Michael giggled. "I think Diana would kill us both if we do that."

Billy thought about it. "Probably true."

Michael said, "I thought about doing it in the Foodland where we met in Hawaii after all those years apart."

"Sounds cheesy, brah."

Michael said, "That's what I thought, too. I'll figure it out. Might be kind of fun to have everyone at the house—my mom, you, Kimberly—after I propose, and we can grill and drink beers."

Billy said, "That would be cool. Just figure out where and when you'll give her that monster rock. Too bad your dad won't be here to see it. I think he was trying to get you back here for years."

Michael thought about what Billy said. "Huh—that's what my mom said last night, too."

Billy, finishing up his burrito, said, "You hear from Isaac?"

"He sent me an email when he got back to base. He told me that we'll go pig hunting again when he gets back after his deployment in six months. He always signs every email, "Love, Isaac." I have even seen him do it with work emails." Imitating Isaac perfectly, Michael said, "*Dear Commander fuck face, after careful consideration, I have determined that you are a fucking asshole. Love, Isaac.*"

Billy laughed a big, deep belly laugh. They got up to leave.

Michael said, "I leave on Thursday, so I'm going to have to propose in the next couple of days. I'll let you know what we figure out."

"Cool, brah."

They walked outside.

"Hey, Billy. If you don't have plans on Thanksgiving, you're welcome to come to the Grands'. Janice and I, and maybe her husband

and kids, will be coming back out in a few weeks. We thought it would be a great way to honor my dad."

Billy said, "Wow, that's great. I think we're going to Kimberly's parents' house, but if we don't, I'll let you know."

They hugged, and Billy went to the station to do some paperwork.

CHAPTER 20

Michael stopped at the fish market and got some fresh Mahi and shrimp. Then he went to the wine store and bought a cult bottle of Paso Robles Syrah, which frankly, he was surprised to see sitting on the shelf in a wine store in tiny Kailua, when he couldn't even get this bottle in Atlanta. Then he went to the supermarket and bought all the ingredients for Caesar Salad. Tonight was going to be grill night at Diana's. Michael went home and unloaded his groceries. Sarah was making soup in the kitchen.

"Hi, Honey. Want some soup?"

"No, thanks, mom. I had lunch with Billy." Michael logged in to the office computer and checked flights. Unfortunately as it was so close to Thanksgiving, tickets were expensive, but it didn't bother Michael, and he booked a flight coming in the day before and leaving the following Sunday. Afterwards, Michael took a nap and woke up hours later. He got ready for dinner and told his mom that he was going over to Diana's house and not to wait up for him. She said that the neighbors had invited her over to dinner and that he shouldn't worry about her.

By the time that Michael went over to Diana's house, she had changed out of her uniform and was wearing jeans and a tight GORUCK t-shirt that accentuated her curves.

"Man, let's skip dinner and go right to the medal round."

Diana looked at him and said, "Silly boy." They kissed.

Michael put the groceries on the counter and made out with Diana for a little bit. "Come on. Let's make dinner."

"What can I do?"

"You can wash and tear up the Romaine lettuce and grate the Parmesan cheese."

"Done. What else can I do?"

"You can put on some music."

Diana turned on her laptop, which had mostly country music in her playlist. Michael went out to Diana's backyard and preheated her grill. As they prepared the salad, they talked about each other's day. Diana, chopping onions said, "This morning at the gym, I heard two guys call me a hot MILF."

Michael laughed. "You *are* a hot MILF. That's quite a compliment."

"I feel old," Diana responded.

Michael said, "I get better with age. I don't feel old. And, besides, I remember a conversation between you and your roommate at BU, the one who didn't believe in wearing underwear."

Diana interrupted him. "*Susan.* Susan had the hots for you. Susan is now a neurosurgeon in Washington, D.C. We still keep in touch."

Michael interjected, "No, she didn't."

Diana responded, "Yes, she did. She told me."

Michael giggled. "Oh! Well, anyway, I remember the discussion that you and Susan had after yoga one day. You told her that you would never feel old."

Diana responded, "Wow! I can't believe that you remember that. Regardless, I feel old."

Michael said, "Well, I still love you, and you *are* a hot MILF."

Diana said, "Thank you, counselor."

During dinner, Michael told Diana about Thanksgiving.

Diana said, "Oh, boy! So that means I get your orgasmic stuffing?"

For years, Michael had made a sourdough-artichoke-parmesan-rosemary stuffing recipe he found in a *Sunset Magazine*. It became the staple of Grand Thanksgivings. Michael said, "Yes, ma'am."

"I signed up for a shift in the ICU on Thanksgiving, but I can be there afterwards, around 7:30."

"That's fine. We can eat a little later. I'll just keep my mom on as my official taste tester throughout the day. She won't mind."

"And, that will mean a few more days together. I'd like that."

"Me, too."

They finished dinner, and then they stripped and went into Diana's wood-fired hot tub, where Michael relearned something that he had forgotten years ago: hot tubs always equal sex. When they were each sufficiently wrinkled, they took a cool shower. Michael told Diana that he would see her tomorrow, and he left. It was a nice night.

Michael woke up before sunrise and took a long walk on the beach. Then he came home and showered and, for the first time in three days, shaved. He put on a pair of slacks and borrowed another one of Joshua's Reyn Spooners. He kissed his mom. Sarah wished him good luck, and Michael drove into Honolulu to meet with Marvin.

The sun was out, so Michael drove up the Pali with the top down. Michael parked in Marvin's building downtown and took the elevator to the 32nd floor. The elevator opened, and he announced himself to the receptionist sitting in the big desk behind a large foyer off of the elevator bay; Wong, Miller, Abernathy, and Konishige had taken over the entire 32nd floor. Michael sat and read a current automobile magazine. A few minutes later, he heard a shriek and a yell: "Hey, *Haole* Boy!" It was Marvin's paralegal, Beth Watanabe. They hugged. "We are all heartbroken about your dad. We all loved him."

"Thanks, Beth."

"How are things in Atlanta? Do you like it there?"

"It's different from Hawaii."

"Do you say '*y'all*' all the time?"

"Hah! Sometimes. You throw it into conversation by habit." Michael continued, "How *y'all*? How's momma dem and *y'all*? How are all *y'all*? If *y'all* don't knock it off, I best be calling me some *po-lice*."

Beth howled. She said, "Come on. Let's take you back to see Marvin. He is excited to talk to you."

Marvin was sitting at his desk.

As senior managing partner, Marvin had the corner office, with huge windows that covered a 180-degree view from Diamond Head on the left to Aloha Tower and downtown in the middle, and, to the right, you could see all the way to West Oahu. Michael always marveled at the view.

"*Boychik!*" Marvin got up from his desk and came over to Michael; they shook hands. Marvin's signature big walrus mustache was a lot grayer, but Marvin was still very much as stylish as Michael remembered. Marvin was something of a clothes horse and would fly to

Hong Kong on a whim just to have shirts and suits made. He was pushing 70 and was still in great shape. He golfed and played tennis three times a week. Michael sat for a bit, and they made small talk. Marvin asked how Sarah was doing.

Michael responded, "Only time will figure that one out. She has good days and bad days. They were married a long time."

Marvin got up out of his office chair and said to Michael, "Come on. Let's go eat. How about Aloha Tower?"

"Great."

They walked the short distance from Marvin's office, chatting and catching up the entire time.

Michael always had a fond place in his heart for Aloha Tower. At one time, it was one of the highest points on the island but had been slowly dwarfed by its high-rise office-building and condo neighbors. Aloha Tower was from another time, a time when Pan Am Clippers from California and cruise ships would de-board there. Over the years, its old glory had faded as the modern jet age arrived, and the tower and the surrounding buildings fell into disrepair. As a young man, Michael had seen a *Social Distortion* concert in one of the old, abandoned luggage terminals at one of the piers at the Aloha Tower. He'd gone to high school with one of the security guards, who let Michael do stage dives for most of the night. In the 1990s, the City of Honolulu allowed a developer to rediscover the area and modernize it with a shopping complex and restaurants. It had an amazing view of the water.

Marvin had a reservation at a restaurant on the water. They sat outside and watched the container ships come in and out of Honolulu Harbor, one of the world's busiest ports. As Michael was eating a grilled Mahi Mahi sandwich, he figured out why Marvin wanted to talk to him. Marvin said, "Michael, you can have your old job back, but I think your talents might be best served somewhere else."

Michael said, between bites of his sandwich, "How?"

Marvin continued. "The Governor needs to appoint a replacement to sit in your dad's chair, and your name came up."

Michael almost choked on his sandwich. He was stunned. "Wait. Marvin, you want me to be a Judge? An *Appellate Court Judge?*"

Marvin said, "Michael, think about it. You're perfectly suited for the job."

Michael continued, "Marvin, I'm a trial lawyer, but I never thought about being a judge. I don't know. I'm not qualified. My dad was a trial judge first for a while before he became an appellate court judge. It was a logical extension of his career. I don't have that experience. Besides, I'm a carpetbagger."

Marvin shot Michael a look of fake indignation. "*Carpetbagger.* Michael, we're not running you for office. You would be a political appointment. The Governor will nominate you."

Michael responded, "Isn't there a nominating committee, vetting, all of those things?"

Marvin had a wry smile. "I sit on the Judicial Selection Commission. There are six names that go on a list that is sent to the Governor. You are interviewing. With me. Right now." Of course, it would be a decent pay cut from what you're making in Atlanta, but your dad turned out alright. Michael, how old are you? Forty-five, right?"

"Yes."

"*Boychik*, how old was your dad when he took the job?"

"Forty-five."

"Thank you."

Michael looked visibly stunned.

Marvin continued. "Over the years, I have learned that the law is a little like *white burgundy*; both really can't be appreciated until you're in your forties. You are a great lawyer, with 20 years of trial experience. You're going to be a great judge, Michael. You're also the perfect age to be an appellate court judge."

Michael got a sudden chill.

Marvin sensed it. "What's wrong?"

Michael said, "My mom told me that my dad was trying for the past six years to get me back here, but he was worried that I would have a big pair of shoes to fill. The irony here is that I will be wearing *his shoes*."

Marvin said, "Michael, it would be a great tribute to your dad— and everyone loved him. My sense is that you will be confirmed. You are still barred here, right?"

"Yes."

Marvin said, "Getting residency is no problem. Michael, your state needs you."

Michael looked at his sandwich and said to Marvin, "I need to think about it. Can I think about it?"

Marvin said, "Yes, but don't think on it too long. The Senate must confirm someone on the list within the next 30 days."

Michael looked at Marvin and said, "What about the other five names?"

Marvin said, "*Boychik*, don't worry about the other five names. Your Uncle Marvin will take care of you." Marvin winked at Michael. Marvin was a political operator of the highest order.

Michael said, "Marvin, sometimes I wonder at the powers of the universe. I was getting burnt out on Atlanta, on the rat race, billable hours, terrible people as clients, all of it. I would have made partner next year, but I don't care anymore."

Marvin smiled ruefully and said to Michael, "*Welcome to the Majors, Mr. Hobbs.*"

Michael giggled. He knew the reference from *The Natural*, which was among both lawyers' favorite movies. Michael thought about Marvin's offer and responded slowly, "I think it would be a great way to honor my dad. I just worry that I wouldn't be very good at it."

Marvin said, "*Boychik*, your dad said the same thing to me when he was nominated."

Michael started to tear up.

Marvin got up from the table, and Michael followed. As they walked out of the restaurant, Marvin stopped, turned to Michael, and said, "Michael, you have tried cases in front of some of the best judges in the country. You know the good ones. You know the Federal Rules of Civil Procedure and the Federal Rules of Evidence, and the state equivalents, cold. You're ready. You'll make a great judge."

Michael said, "Marvin, give me 24 hours. I have some thinking to do."

Marvin said, "*Boychik*, you have yourself a deal." The two shook hands. They walked back to Marvin's office, and Michael took the elevator to his car.

CHAPTER 21

Michael drove home, giddy. He kept replaying the meeting with Marvin. He was thinking about what Marvin had said. It occurred to Michael, though, that the curvy, wet road of the Pali Highway was not the best place to be thinking about his life and that he needed to concentrate on driving. He turned up the radio, shifted into second, and sped up. Traffic was light, so he took the deep curves at speed. Growing up in Hawaii, every driver knows how to drive on wet roads. Out of the tunnel, Michael drifted through the steepest turns on the Kailua side of the road, more feeling the road than driving it. The 280SL was responding in kind. It was a driver's car, and it loved to be driven. By the time Michael had reached Kailua town, the rain had stopped. The drive had cleared his head, but he was still giddy.

Michael pulled the car into the driveway. The late-afternoon sun cast long shadows on the front grass. He went to lie on an old green hammock tied between two large coconut trees that were almost original to the house. He lay there with his hands behind his neck, watched the clouds move in the sky, and listened to the doves cooing on the ground next to the hammock. There was a nice breeze rustling the leaves of the mango tree and the palm fronds. Michael started to think.

Sarah came out with a glass of iced tea. Sarah handed Michael the glass and sat on the edge of the hammock. "Hi, Honey. How did it go with Marvin?"

Michael said, "Funny you should ask. He wants me to apply for dad's old job."

Sarah said, "Oh, wow! That would be quite an honor."

Michael propped himself up on one arm and said, "That's what Marvin thinks, too."

Sarah put her arm around Michael's shoulders and said, "What do you think?"

Michael said, "I think it would be a great way to remember my dad, but I worry that I wouldn't be any good at the job. I worry that if I take it, people, over time, will begin to forget dad and that I will eclipse him."

Sarah told her son, "Michael, it would give your dad great happiness to know that you still care and think about him that way."

Michael responded, "Mom, there isn't a moment in the day where I don't think about him."

Sarah said, "Michael, your dad was a mighty big tree. Big trees stay around for a long time."

Michael asked his mom, "Do you think I should accept?"

Sarah started to tear up and said, "Yes. Yes, I do."

Michael said, "I told Marvin that I would think about it and get back to him tomorrow. Marvin said that I would be on a list with five other names and that, once there was a nomination, the Senate would take 30 days to confirm. I guess I am going to have to speed up my timetable for coming back here."

At that moment, tears of sadness and happiness poured down Sarah's cheeks. They hugged.

Michael texted Diana, and she responded immediately. "I've been thinking about you all day. How did it go?"

"Take me to dinner and I'll tell you . . ."

"Deal. I will pick U up around 6:30. Buzz's?"

"Can't ever have enough Buzz's . . ."

"K. Luv U."

"Luv U."

Michael went for a quick swim in the ocean, walked the beach a little, turned around, and showered in the outside shower. He wrapped his towel around his waist and went into his bedroom to change. Michael borrowed another Reyn Spooner from his dad's huge collection of aloha shirts in his dad's closet. He grabbed the blue *Lahaina Trader* Spooner, probably the most famous and recognizable pattern of all Reyn Spooners. He would ask his mom if he could have some of his dad's aloha shirts, as they were the *de rigeur* uniform of professional men in Hawaii. Except for lawyers in court, most businessmen in Hawaii wore a Reyn Spooner to work. Michael put on his driving shoes without socks, put on his Dad's Rolex, and sprayed himself with his dad's Aqua di Gio cologne. *I'm becoming my dad*, Michael thought. Michael Grand was honored to become Joshua Grand.

At 6:30, Diana's LS 400 pulled up in the driveway. Michael was waiting outside. He saw Diana pull up, walked to the car, and got into the passenger side. Diana waved. Diana was wearing a simple black cocktail dress. Diana reached over, and they kissed. Diana drove the short distance from the Grand house to Buzz's. As they pulled in, Michael noticed that, on the flagpole, there was a flag for *Hebi*, the Shortbill Spearfish. It was on the menu, and it was Michael's personal favorite. They held hands from the car.

Diana asked him, "*So?* You're killing me. What happened?"

Michael told Diana, "Marvin is going to nominate me to fill the vacancy left on the Hawaii Court of Appeals when my dad died."

Diana stopped walking, looked right into Michael's eyes, and said, "Michael, that's the most amazing thing that I have ever heard. It would be a tremendous honor to your dad. Are you going to accept?"

Michael responded, "I think so. I have to think on it for a bit more. The pluses far outweigh the minuses."

Diana looked at Michael and asked, "What are the pluses?"

Michael looked at Diana and said, "*You.*"

Diana started to tear up, and Michael continued, "I lost you once before. I don't want to go through that again." Michael stopped walking and just stood there; he said to Diana, "You know, I was racking my brain on when do to this, trying to come up with some elaborate plan, but I'm just going to do this. I've been carrying this thing around with me for the past couple of days." Michael reached into his pocket and pulled out the red ring box. Diana looked mortified.

"Michael, what's happening?"

Michael got down on one knee.

Diana said, "Oh!" and put her hands to her face.

Michael, with a smile on his face, said, "Diana Jane Eisenberg, will you marry me?"

Diana started crying and said, "Yes!"

Michael didn't realize that he had just proposed in front of the restaurant, and people waiting outside for their tables started clapping and cheering. He put the ring on Diana's finger and said, "I hope it fits. I had to guess at your size."

Diana looked at the ring in the light from the streetlamp above. Even in the dark, it sparkled. She said, "That is some ring. You've always had good taste."

Michael said, "You deserve it. I'm crazy about you. You're the best thing that ever happened to me."

Diana beamed.

Buzz's was busy, and they had to wait almost an hour for their table. People waiting outside for their tables kept buying Michael and Diana drinks. Diana kept sneaking peeks at the ring.

Michael would remember this day for a very long time.

Diana pulled into the Grands' driveway, turned off the engine, and they just sat there for a minute. Michael got out of the car and beckoned for Diana to follow him to the hammock. They lay on the hammock together under the moonlight, the wind gently blowing. Michael asked his fiancée, "Are you happy?"

Diana responded, almost dreamily, "Yes."

Michael said, "I'm glad. Do you like the ring?"

"No, Michael—I *love* the ring."

Michael, lost in his own thoughts, interrupted Diana and said, "If you don't like it, I can get something bigger."

Diana poked Michael in the ribs and said, "Michael, I love the ring. And, I love you."

Michael said, "I love you, too."

They stayed there for what felt like hours, but, in reality, it was only about 45 minutes. Diana was asleep, with a smile on her face.

Michael woke her up. "Hey, baby. Let's go to bed."

"Okay," Diana said sleepily.

They quietly entered the house, trying not to wake up Sarah, and they stripped and got quietly into bed. Diana instantly fell back asleep, and Michael was not far behind her.

Michael woke up at dawn and carefully extricated himself from his bed without waking up his fiancée. He sent an email to Isaac. *Proposed to Diana last night. She said yes. We'll make wedding plans when you return. My old boss wants to nominate me to fill dad's position on the bench. I'm thinking I'm going to accept. Stay safe. M*

Diana left to go home and get ready for work but told Michael that they would talk later in the day. Michael texted Billy and asked if he was free for lunch. Billy texted back that he was, that he would meet him at Boots & Kimo's at noon.

CHAPTER 22

Michael and Sarah walked the beach and stopped for coffee afterwards at Kalapawai. Sarah was thrilled about the events of the past day. She told her son, "I'm happy to welcome Diana into the family. She's a lovely young woman."

"Thanks, mom. I think she'll fit in nicely with the rest of us *Meshugahs*."

Sarah laughed and said, "We have always prided ourselves in how big we live life. We love with big hearts, are tolerant of each other, *forgive* each other, and live with a sense that we have lived to the fullest. I think that Diana will work just fine. I just wish that your dad was around to see you two get married. That is all he wanted for years."

"Dad will be there. I know it."

Michael met Billy at Boots & Kimo's. Michael had the Pakalolo Onolicious Omelet, and Billy had the Mochiko Chicken.

Michael told Billy about proposing to Diana.

Billy reached across the table and high-fived Michael. Michael then told him about being nominated for his dad's open seat on the bench, and Billy said loudly, in the middle of the restaurant, "Fucking nepotism!"

Michael giggled.

Billy told Michael that he was thrilled for him, that he and Kimberly had better be invited to the wedding. Michael said that they would have seats saved in the front row for the two of them.

As they were leaving, Billy said, "It's been a hell of week for Michael Grand."

Michael said, "You're telling *me*."

Billy said, "I'm thrilled for you."

They hugged. Michael told Billy that he would try to see him one more time before he left the next night and that he would be back in a couple of weeks.

Michael called Marvin Chong. "Marvin, after careful consideration, I have decided to accept the honor of being nominated to fill my dad's seat on the Hawaii Court of Appeals."

Marvin said, with excitement in his voice, "*Boychik*, this is good news. I think you've made the right decision. I'll be in touch with you about the next steps."

Sarah was marinating chicken in a teriyaki sauce and making some assorted salads. She looked up as Michael walked in and asked her son, "Do you and Diana want to come with me to the yacht club tonight to grill and sit by Kaneohe Bay?"

Michael said, "I would love to. I will see if my fiancée will want to come."

Sarah smiled at Michael's use of the word "fiancée."

Michael texted Diana, and she responded that she would love to join them, that she would meet at the house about six. He checked his email. There was a response from Isaac, who was probably just getting up from a long night. *Michael, in Special Operations, they teach you that when you fight, you fight for only the things that matter. Diana matters, and you fought for something important. I'm glad that you proposed to that good woman. I'm thrilled for you. You will make a great judge, Your Honor. Dad would have been proud. Love, Isaac.*

Diana came over after work. She was wearing jeans and a Peacemaker Trading Company t-shirt. She had a BU hockey sweatshirt tied around her waist. She hugged Sarah, and she and Michael kissed. They helped Sarah load the food into Diana's trunk, and they all piled into Diana's LS 400 and drove to the yacht club in neighboring Kaneohe.

The yacht club, established in 1924, was the oldest continuously operating harbor facility and club house to promote seamanship in the State of Hawaii. The yacht club was where countless generations of Hawaii's youth had learned to sail on summer breaks, Michael included.

Joshua's fishing boat, the *Res Ipsa*, was also docked there. In law, *Res Ipsa Loquitor* is a term meaning *"The thing speaks for itself"* and is used to prove negligence. Sarah had a love-hate relationship with the *Res Ipsa* and usually referred to the boat as ". . . Joshua's mistress. . . ." Joshua loved to fish, though, and he often brought Sarah and the kids on Sunday outings to the local sandbar, or past it, fishing up the coast, near Haleiwa. The kids loved the boat, and she provided a lifetime of memories for the Grands over the years.

Sarah found a nice table near the water. There were a few people mulling around, with a small gathering busily tending to the centerpiece of their dinners at the large communal grill. Sarah asked to see Diana's hand and said, "That's a beautiful ring."

Diana replied, "Your son did good."

Sarah said, "He has good taste, just like his father."

Michael said, "Mom, you're going to make me blush in front of my newly minted fiancée."

Sarah went off and got drinks at the bar, Hinanos for Diana and Michael and a glass of Malbec for herself. Diana and Michael were sitting next to each other and holding hands when she returned.

"Beers for the two love birds."

Michael got up to grill the chicken. Sarah and Diana stayed at the table talking. Michael heard the two of them laughing and realized that this was the first time since his dad had died that he had heard his mom laugh. He missed his mom's laugh, which came from deep in her belly and roared out. It was pure and genuine.

After dinner, they went to go sit on the *Res Ips*a.

Sarah rubbed the hull and said, "Joshua loved this boat."

Michael said, "We had lots of good times on her."

Diana said, "I remember once we all went out and were fishing off of the marine base. Your dad said, 'Log!' He steered for it, and we hit a school of Mahi Mahi. I loved how, as soon as they came out of the water, they turned from blue to gold. That was when your dad said, 'That's why Mahi are also called El Dorado.'"

Michael said, "We must have caught a dozen Mahi on that trip. I don't remember ever working so hard as we did that day."

Diana said, "Your dad said that I could steer since I was in the Navy. He and you and Isaac were fishing like mad dogs. Practically every time a line went in the water, you would haul up another fish."

Sarah said, "We ate Mahi for weeks after that. I actually got sick of Mahi Mahi for a while."

Michael said, "Mom, remember the time when we were kids, fishing, and a bunch of flying fish flew into the boat? Janice and Isaac were catching them with their bare hands."

Sarah said, "I do. You were trying to throw as many back as possible. A lot of good memories on this boat."

Michael said, "I'm glad that she's staying in the family."

Sarah looked at Michael and told her son, "You and your brother are going to have to help me keep her up. She needs a lot of maintenance."

Michael said, "We will, mom."

Michael woke up with the sunrise. Diana woke up, too.

"Good morning."

"Good morning."

Michael said, "How did you sleep?"

Diana turned over, looked at Michael, and said, "Michael, when we get married, can you promise me that we will get a larger bed?"

Michael giggled and said, "Yes, dear."

They spent the next half-an-hour lying in bed, holding hands and talking softly. Diana got out of bed, threw on the clothes that she'd worn the night before, and bent over to kiss Michael, who was still in bed. She said, "I have to go home and get ready for work. The nice thing about being in the Navy is that a girl doesn't have to go home and go through her closet to figure out what she's going to wear. All she has to do is throw on her uniform and go."

Michael said, "Go and leave me in peace, sailor. I'll call you later. I love you."

"I love you, too"

Michael got out of bed, and he and Sarah walked the beach for the last time until he would come back for Thanksgiving. Michael spent the day hanging around the house, doing laundry and listening to his iPod. Diana called him and said that she was working at the clinic at Kaneohe, that she had only a few Marines to see, and that she wanted to know if they could have lunch. Michael said that he would love to have lunch with the future Mrs. Grand.

CHAPTER 23

Diana picked Michael up at noon and said that she didn't have much time. So they went to a supermarket and bought a pound of *Ahi Shoyu Poke* and a half-pound of *Ahi Limu Poke*, a loaf of fresh-baked sourdough bread, and a couple of bottles of water. They went to Kailua Beach Park to have lunch at a picnic table.

Diana said, sadly, "I'm going to miss you."

Michael said, "Me, too. It's just for a couple of weeks. I'll call, text, email, or facetime you every day. I have to head back for the trial, which should conclude early next week. I thought that I was coming out here to bury my dad and leave. If I'd thought that I was also going to propose to the woman of my dreams, I most certainly would have planned this better and stayed longer."

Diana giggled, "Hah! This has been a fucking whirlwind tour, man. I have fallen for a guy fast in the past, but this might be my personal record."

Michael laughed and asked Diana, "Did your girlfriends like the ring?"

Diana snickered at him and said, "Michael, we don't just sit around and twirl our hair and compare diamond sizes. I'm a busy person with a life, but yes, the two or three women at work I showed it to thought I did very well."

Michael said, "Did you ever think that we would be getting married?"

Diana looked at him and said, "Michael, you are my soul mate. It took me a while to figure that out, but I always held onto the dream of marrying you."

Michael said, "Oh, good. Just don't cheat on me again."

Diana said, "Michael, I love you and want to spend the rest of my life with you. Thank you for taking me back."

Michael sighed and said, "Well, I'm glad we got *that* out of the way."

Diana told Michael, "I almost didn't go to your dad's funeral. I sat in the car in the parking lot of the cemetery and almost didn't go in."

Michael responded, "Why?"

Diana told him, "Because I didn't want to hurt you anymore." She started crying.

Michael said, "I'm certainly happy that you came to my dad's funeral. We wouldn't be here now if you hadn't."

Diana smiled and said, "You're right."

Michael, thinking to himself, blurted out, "Huh."

Diana said, "What?"

"Motherfucker!"

"Michael, *what*?"

Michael had a smile on his face and said, "My dad got us together. If it wasn't for him, I would have never come back out here, and I would have spent the rest of my life wondering about you. He wanted us to get back together, and he made it happen. Son of a bitch. I feel like he is watching down from up there and smiling." Michael looked up to heaven and said, "Thank you, dad!"

Michael looked over at Diana. She was still crying. Michael was concerned and said, "Are you upset?"

Diana said, "No, Michael. I'm happy. I'm very happy." Diana looked up to heaven, too, and said, "Thank you, Joshua."

Sarah made Michael dinner. They sat at the table. Sarah told her son, "I'm so glad you came out for the funeral. I could not have done this without you."

Michael, holding his mom's hand, said, "It was the least I could have done. Sad time. Happy time. All at the same time. Crazy week."

Sarah, with her years of age and wisdom under her belt, replied, "That's life, Honey. The good and the bad are intertwined."

Michael asked his mom, "Are you going to be okay for a few weeks until I can get back?"

His mom said, "Yes. The house will be very quiet, but I'll use the time to think about your dad. I'll be okay. I have some really good friends I can resume a relationship with as I step into a life without your dad. There is a grief-therapy group at the hospital. I think I'll join it. Queen's wants me to come back, part time, to do shifts in the ER. My license is still current. I've kept up my certifications. I retired when your dad got sick to take care of him. Now, I need to take care of *me*."

Michael, a little surprised said, "Wow, mom! That's great, but do you want to do that?"

Sarah nodded and said, "It will be a good distraction."

Michael's mom had always been one of his role models. He said, "Mom, I've always looked up to your inner strength."

Sarah said, "The Grands are all strong. Your dad was strong. Isaac is strong. Janice is strong. You're strong. This has been our most redeeming quality."

They hugged.

Sarah said, "You're a good man, Charlie Brown."

Michael said, "Mom, I'll see you in a few weeks."

Sarah said, "I love you."

Michael said, "I love you, too"

Billy drove Michael to the airport. Many HPD officers used their personal vehicles as their duty vehicles. It made life interesting for teenagers and criminals who think that, because there are no police vehicles visible, there are no cops around. In reality, there's always a cop around. Billy had his own car that he used on duty, but he picked Michael up in a squad car and made Michael sit in back. He put Michael's luggage in the trunk.

When Billy drove off, Michael said from the back, "On, James."

Billy said, "I am going to have my buddies at TSA strip-search you and give you a full rectal examination. Brah, I'm going to miss you."

Michael said, "Don't make me sad. I'll be gone only a few weeks. I'm coming back for Thanksgiving. Maybe longer, if the universe wants me here."

Billy said to his friend, "Michael, you're coming back here. The universe wants you here."

"Thanks, buddy."

Billy said, "Oh, I checked with Kimberly. She said that, if we can bring the kids, she would love to come to the Grands' for Thanksgiving."

Michael responded, "I'll check with my mom, but I don't think that will be a problem."

They drove and talked through the bulletproof divider.

Billy said, "Definitely a wild week."

Michael, curious about how his friend had known to pull him over said, "Hey, Bill. How did you know that I was back in town? I didn't call you."

Billy responded with a smile on his face, "Your mom called me."

Michael said, "Of course, she did."

Billy said to his friend, "I'm glad we were able to re-connect. We've known each other so long that we can go without seeing each other for long durations, and, when we get back together, I still feel like we're fifteen years old."

Billy pulled the HPD cruiser up to the departures area at HNL and parked the car. Michael got out, and Billy grabbed his luggage.

Michael said, "Besides Isaac, Janice, my mom, and now, Diana, you are the only family I have here. Thank you for that."

"You are most welcome, brah."

They hugged.

"Safe flight, Mike"

"Give my love to Kimberly and the boys, and tell them I'll see them in a few weeks."

CHAPTER 24

The flight into Hartsfield was bumpy. It was early afternoon by the time he stepped out into the cold Atlanta day. Michael shivered. Hawaii had thinned his blood in a week. He was tired. He took an Uber car home to his condo; a nice kid from Georgia Tech was the driver, trying to earn a little extra money between classes. Michael collected his mail, showered, shaved, and then went off to Harry's Farmer's Market in Marietta to get some food for the week. He wanted to be back in Kailua with Diana. He missed her. He missed his mom. He missed Isaac. He missed Janice.

Michael came home and watched some TV on his couch. Then he called Diana, and they spoke, but she was between patients, and she couldn't talk for very long.

Diana asked him, "How was the flight?"

Michael, tiredly, said, "It was good. I upgraded to San Francisco, but I didn't sleep much." Michael could never really sleep on Red Eye flights, and this one was no different, despite noise-cancelling headphones, a business-class seat, wine, and dinner.

Diana said, "Well, I have to go do a treadmill on a SEAL who is having chest pain when he swims. I think his days of rootin' and tootin', shootin', and parachutin' are over."

Michael got the reference and said, "Clever girl. Next time we're in bed, you have to recite the *Ballad of the Frogman* to me. It'll really turn me on."

Diana said, "Deal. Goodnight, my love. Sleep well."

Michael said, "Goodnight, sailor girl. You have a good evening."

Diana said, "I will. Love you."

"I love you, too." Michael hung up the phone, and the next thing he remembered was the sun coming through his condo window the next morning.

Michael spent Saturday and Sunday getting into trial mode, going over testimony, evidence, police reports, plotting strategy. Often during trials, he wouldn't let anything distract him. He became completely focused on his client. This time, though, it was hard to concentrate as his mind wandered and leapt from one thought to another—his dad, his love for Diana, concern for his mom and Janice. He thought about his brother serving in a faraway place. He emailed Isaac, texted Diana, called his mom, and texted Janice. They all responded.

Michael didn't leave his apartment all weekend. On Monday, he put on his favorite suit that he and his dad had gotten in Hong Kong many years ago, put on his favorite Hermès tie, a blue dress shirt, his favorite cufflinks, and his dad's Rolex. He climbed into his Mercedes G63 for the quick drive to the Fulton County Superior Court building. Michael's dad had been a Mercedes guy, and, thus, Michael was a Mercedes guy. The G63 had been Michael's only lavish spend on himself. He'd bought it when he moved to Atlanta. He truly loved the big, boxy SUV. While the new version had a twin turbo and was a bit faster than his, he loved naturally aspirated engines, and, more importantly, it was long paid off.

Traffic was horrible this morning, and it took him almost 30 minutes from his condo. Usually, he could make the drive in roughly half that time.

Michael's client was waiting for him in front of the courtroom, pacing like an expecting father. He was glad to see that the kid had listened to him and was wearing a suit and had taken the earrings out of his ears. Over the years, Michael had learned that juries like to see clean-cut defendants.

The trial proceeded from where it left off. They were through *voir dire*, and the jury was seated when Michael was granted the continuance. The first thing Michael did was file a Motion *In Limine* to have the blood evidence excluded for being obtained in an illegal search. Michael might not have been the smartest lawyer, but he was certainly one of the best prepared. In Michael's research the weekend before the trial, he discovered that the prosecution was sitting on a significant error. When his client was taken to the hospital after the accident, law enforcement went to the Emergency Room and demanded that they release his blood without a warrant. They threatened the ER staff with arrest until a nurse begrudgingly walked into his client's exam room, drew vials of blood, and handed them to the officers, who were waiting in the nurse's station.

The prosecutor objected to the timing of the Motion *In Limine*. Typically, these types of motions are usually filed pre-trial, but they can be filed after a trial starts. Michael apologized to the court and stated that he was just given this case the day before trial when his client fired his previous attorney. Michael argued that he did not have a chance to file the motion pre-trial and was now only getting back into the case after the continuance had been granted. The judge granted Michael's motion. His client's blood evidence and results were ruled inadmissible and could not be introduced at trial. The prosecutor was fuming.

Michael was not done. After the prosecutor called law enforcement to testify as to the events just after the accident, Michael performed an excellent cross-examination. The officer at the scene testified that they had found his client and his client's friend sitting on the side of the road next to the Porsche. As Michael's client had fled the scene of the crash, Michael asked the officers at the scene if they were able to determine if his client was actually driving the car. The officer read from the accident report that the car pulled over a few miles away from the accident. After the accident, the Porsche was wrecked and not drivable because of significant front-end damage, but the car was able to continue down the road until the damage from the front end caused the left front tire to flatten and strip away from the rim. The Porsche belonged to his client's father.

Michael's client was found by law enforcement sitting on the curb on the driver's side of the car. The assumption was that Michael's client was the driver because his client had the car keys in his hand at the time, and it was his client's father's car. Michael's client refused to answer any questions asked by the officers. Michael asked the arresting officer if the keys in his client's hand were later fingerprinted. The officer said they were not. Michael then asked the officer if it was possible that his client's friend was driving the Porsche at the time of the accident and had given the keys back to Michael's client before they came upon the car.

The officer testified that this was possible, yes. Michael then asked the officer if he physically examined his client after the accident, and the officer indicated that he had not examined his client but that he was taken by ambulance to the ER and that they had examined him and photographed all injuries. Michael was able to subpoena his client's medical records and his client's friend's medical records and had access to the photographs in question. He enlarged these photographs and introduced them as evidence. Michael presented these photographs to the testifying officer and asked the officer if he noticed any wounds to his client. Michael said to the officer that if his client was driving and he'd indeed run the Porsche into the pedestrian with enough force to cause severe front-end damage, either the deploying airbags would have caused facial and knuckle burns to his client, or, had the airbag not deployed, there would have been a substantial bruise to his client's chest where it would have impacted with the steering wheel.

Michael produced the photographs of his client taken during the examination in the ER and asked the testifying officer if he noticed any bruises or injuries on his client's person. The officer testified that he could not find any evidence of injuries on his client's chest, hands, or face. Then, Michael presented the photographs of his client's friend taken when he was examined in the same ER by the same doctors, and he asked the law-enforcement officer what he saw. The officer on the stand testified that Michael's client's friend had deep bruising on both his chest and face. Michael asked the officer if he believed if it was possible that his client might not have been driving. The officer agreed that it was possible that Michael's client might not have been driving the Porsche on the night of the accident.

The rest of the trial was relatively easy, and the defense rested without calling any witnesses. Michael had succeeded in getting crucial evidence thrown out and raised enough reasonable doubt that, after one hour of deliberation, the jury came back with a "Not Guilty" verdict.

Michael's client reached over and said "Thank you" to Michael.

Michael told his client, "I didn't do it for you," which left his client with a perplexed look on his face. Michael Grand wanted to win the last case he was ever going to be involved with as an attorney.

He immediately left the courthouse and drove home. On the way, he thought to himself, *How nice it would be if this was indeed the last case I would ever try*, and a little smile appeared on his face.

CHAPTER 25

Michael later called Diana when she was driving home from work. He didn't like to talk to her while she was driving because Diana refused to buy a new car, and the old LS 400 had been made at a time when drivers generally did not talk on their phones. He told her that he would call her a little later.

Diana called him when she got home. Diana asked, "Hi. How are you? How is my favorite man-child?"

Michael responded, "Hi. Good. Things are good. I just finished my case. As I was driving home, I decided that this would be my last case as a lawyer. I'm done being a litigator. It takes too much out of me. If I don't get the judge job, I'll figure something else out."

Diana was very supportive. She said, "Wow! That's very forward thinking. Did you win?"

Michael said, "I did. That kid walked out of the courthouse a free man. He was looking at Manslaughter. That part was gratifying, but he is an asshole." Michael rarely told anyone outside of other lawyers what he thought about his clients.

Diana, one of Michael's biggest fans, said, "Well, I still love you."

Michael asked, "Did you have a crazy day?"

Diana said, "Not too bad. I was going to go to Buzz's for lunch, but I don't have my Buzz's buddy."

Michael said, "Baby, I will take you to Buzz's every day for lunch, if that's what you want." Diana responded, "Nah. That place is special to me. I don't want to deplete its power by going there all the time."

"Good answer, sailor."

"What's on the docket for this evening, counselor?"

Michael said, "I'm probably going to walk to Lennox Square Mall and wander around for a while, grab some dinner, come home. It's not far."

Diana, said, playfully, "That sounds a little boring. Do you want me to come visit?"

Michael said, "Um, how fast can you get here?"

Following up, Diana said, "Let's see, if I go home and pack, I could probably get the last flight out to the coast. I could be there by the middle of tomorrow."

Michael said, sincerely, "Too long."

Diana laughed and said, "Well, I'll see you in little more than a week. That will be nice."

Michael said, "It'll be the beginning of the rest of our lives together. I am done with moving to places far and away. I want to come home."

Diana continued, "We haven't talked about where we'll live."

Michael, thinking about it said, "Wow! You're right!"

Diana asked Michael, "Want to move in with me? My house might not be on the water, but it's close to your mom's, and it does have that awesome wood-fired hot tub that we seemed to enjoy the last time we used it."

Michael said, "I haven't really thought about where I'm going to live. I guess I can't live at my mom's forever. I would love to move in with you. I'm not going to be making what I make here, but I'll still be doing okay. I can more than contribute. As a sign of my intent, I'll ship my car there."

Diana said, "That sounded very officious, counselor."

Michael said, "I am a very officious guy, Doctor."

Diana said, "Well, that's what I love about you."

Michael responded, "I thought you loved my boyish charm and good looks."

Diana said, "I love those, too. Have you heard from Isaac?"

Michael had been thinking about his brother. "We talk by email. He ends his deployment in six months, I wonder what he'll do. He's getting pretty old to be still kicking in doors."

Diana asked, "He has been in 16, right?"

Michael said, "I think so. He definitely wants to get to his 20."

"I'll have to look around and see if we can find him something at Tripler, I know people there, you know."

Michael giggled, "Hah! I know. That would be great, if he wants it."

Diana said, "Okay, I've just noticed that I'm starving, I didn't have lunch. Go enjoy your evening—you deserve it."

Michael said, "Talk tomorrow?"

"Of course."

"Love you."

"Love you, too."

The next day, Michael gave his notice to his firm, much to their surprise. He thanked them for giving a great opportunity to advance his career when they'd hired him six years prior. When the managing partner asked why Michael was leaving, Michael just responded that it was time for a change, that he was relocating back to Hawaii to pursue other options there. Michael said that he would stay on to the end of the week to wind down or re-assign the other cases that he was working on.

Michael went to work out at his gym and gave them notice that he was terminating his membership because he was moving. Michael had pre-paid for the year, and he told the gym to forward any refund to his mom's house in Hawaii.

Then he went home and reviewed his mail. In the pile was a notice from his landlord that his annual rental agreement was set to expire on January 1st. Michael called his landlord and gave her his 30-day notice of intent to vacate the premises but that he would actually vacate his apartment right before Thanksgiving and that his landlord could advertise to rent it out. His landlord was a little upset. Michael had been a great tenant. He made no messes; he was quiet, he never threw loud parties, and he always paid his rent in full and early. But she wished him well in the next chapter in his life.

In reality, Michael wasn't home to enjoy his apartment much because he was always working. When he moved away from Hawaii, he threw himself into his work. If he wasn't in trial or at the gym, he was at the firm. He was always the first one to arrive at his desk and one of the last to leave. Michael didn't have much furniture—he had a bed, a night table, a dresser, a desk, a couch, a flat-screen TV, and a kitchen table. Michael called Habitat for Humanity and scheduled a pickup for the donation of his furniture and kitchen supplies. Then he called a car shipper and arranged to have the G63 picked up for transport to Hawaii. He prepaid for the shipping over the phone. Then, he went to U-Haul and purchased boxes for shipping his clothes to Hawaii. He didn't have many clothes in Atlanta—five suits, twenty dress shirts, a few pair of slacks, some jeans, some sweaters, casual shirts, an overcoat, an old North Face jacket that he'd had since BU, a few pairs of shoes. An outsider looking in would have determined that Michael hadn't planned on staying in Atlanta very long.

Actually, the six years spent there was a bit of a surprise to Michael. He thought that he would have moved on long ago, but the work and the pay were good, and he was able to gain a lot of valuable experience. After work, he would pack up his clothes and drop the boxes off at the UPS Store prior to work the next day for shipment to his mom's house.

On the last Friday that Michael worked in Atlanta, his firm threw him a goodbye reception in the private room at a nearby restaurant. Most of the office showed up, thanked Michael for his contribution, and told them that he was a great lawyer, that they loved working with him, and that they would miss him. In truth, he had enjoyed working with many of them, too, and would miss the professional relationships going forward. He left his colleagues with an open invitation to come visit, bid everyone farewell, walked into the cold Atlanta night, got his car from the valet, and drove to his condo.

CHAPTER 26

Michael decided that he would spend his last week in the South exploring the South, because he had the luxury of time, something he had not had during his six-year tenure in Atlanta. He moved out of his condo at the end of the week. He drove the 70 miles to Athens, staying for two days. He walked around UGA and went to concerts at the legendary Georgia Theater and the 40-Watt Club. He had dinner at 5&10 and at the National, had lunch at Marti's at Midday, had the best barbeque he had eaten at Weaver D's, whose slogan, *Automatic for the People*, was given a high tribute by R.E.M in the album of the same name. Michael stayed at a hotel in town and loved walking around the Antebellum and post-Civil War buildings downtown. He spent hours buying CDs at Wuxtry Records. He ate breakfast every morning at the Big City Bread Café. Michael told himself that he would love to spend more time in the sleepy little college town that had such a great vibe.

Michael then drove the G63 down to Charleston for two days, ate dinner at FIG, toured the Battery, ate at the community table in Henry's with some really neat people; they closed down the place and went for cocktails afterward. Michael went into one of the oldest synagogues in America, took the ferry in the pouring rain to Fort Sumter, and was amazed at how very small it was in real life. He ate at cafés and small restaurants, bought a seersucker suit at Ben Silver because he'd always wanted a bonafide seersucker suit with his initials embroidered in the lining, like a true Southern gentleman. He fell in love with the quaint, Old World charm of the place and vowed that he would return one day, hopefully, with Diana.

Michael drove back down to Atlanta the day before he was to board the airplane to Hawaii and handed the keys to the G63 to the car-shipping company truck driver, who met him in front of the Westin at Hartsfield International. He bid his car safe travels, thanked and tipped the truck driver, took his luggage into the hotel, and checked in for the night. On Michael's last night in Atlanta, he had a low-key meal at the hotel restaurant, went upstairs to watch the movie channels for a few hours, watched the Atlanta news for the last time, talked with Diana on the phone and told her that he would see her tomorrow, called his mom and told her that he would see her as well, and went to bed early, since he had to get up at 5:30 AM so that he would leave himself enough time to get his 8 AM flight. He knew how crazy the security line at Hartsfield could be on a weekday before Thanksgiving.

Excitement woke Michael up an hour earlier than the alarm was set to go off, and it was still dark outside. He opened the curtains and looked out of the window, down onto the headlights of the traffic on I-85 below. Even at the early hour, there was a steady stream of traffic. He felt the large bay window; it was cold to the touch. Michael went down to the hotel gym for a quick workout. He showered and shaved, threw on a pair of jeans, his dad's watch, running shoes, polo shirt and jacket, checked out, and took the hotel shuttle to the departures terminal.

Once he was through security, he grabbed a quick breakfast at the only non-chain-looking restaurant he could find, got a latte at Starbucks, stopped at a bookstand and got a paperback for the flight, and walked casually to his gate. They called for boarding, and Michael Grand unceremoniously left the city that had been his home for the past six years, ready to start his journey to a new world, to home.

The flight over the ocean was crowded with those lucky enough to be able to be spending Thanksgiving in Hawaii, but it was quiet and uneventful. Michael was able to upgrade, and he listened to music on his iPod through his noise-cancelling headphones and read his paperback. He would track the plane's progress through the GPS program on the screen in front of him, and he would periodically tell himself that he was only a few thousand miles from home. He started getting excited when the screen indicated that he was a few hundred miles from home, as he knew that he would be landing very shortly. When the plane landed on the reef runway extension that jutted out into the Pacific Ocean at Honolulu International Airport, he knew that he was home for good.

He took his time collecting his belongings and let everyone rush off the plane in front of him. Michael took the escalator down to the baggage-claim area to get his bags, and he saw Diana waiting for him with a beautiful tuberose and tea-leaf lei that she had purchased at one of the airport lei stands a few minutes earlier. She was in her service khaki uniform.

Michael looked very surprised. "I never told you what flight I was coming in on. I was going to take a cab and show up at your house." They kissed.

Diana winked and said, "I kind of figured out what flight you were on. It wasn't hard. I wanted to surprise you."

Michael said, "You always were the smart one. Nice surprise." Michael grabbed his luggage, and he and Diana held hands out to the car parked in the parking garage.

On the way home, they made small talk. They stopped for dinner in Honolulu and then went home to Diana's house. They sat out on Diana's lanai for a while and talked. Then they showered together and went to bed.

Michael was dreaming that he and his dad were driving in the 280SL. It was raining, but they had the top down, and both of them were soaked. His dad was smiling. There were no sounds of wind or rain—only of the engine racing. The dream woke Michael up, and he sat up at looked at the clock on the nightstand table. It was 3:37 AM.

Diana woke up and stared at Michael. "Is everything okay?"

Michael said, "Go back to sleep, baby. I was just having a dream."

Diana was a physician in the US Navy, meaning that she could fall asleep anywhere instantaneously—at the movies, on the car wash line, sometimes even standing up.

Michael looked over at Diana. She already was fast asleep. Michael stared at the ceiling for the next two hours and then fell back asleep for an hour.

Diana woke him up when she got up. "Lover boy, you can stay here all day and scour my house to find my deepest and darkest secrets, but that sounds a little creepy. Can I take you over to your mom's? I bet she would want to see you."

Michael propped himself up on an elbow. "You can. I'll go over there and get the car. Today is the food-shopping day in anticipation of Thanksgiving. Plus I should go to Costco. It's going to be a busy day."

Diana was putting on her uniform and said, "I can't wait to eat that fucking stuffing. I've been thinking about it for weeks."

Michael said, "Yep—that's one of my favorites. Do you know I haven't cooked for or celebrated Thanksgiving in the six years that I was in Atlanta?"

Diana was a little surprised by Michael's statement and said, "*What?* You love to cook. *Why?*"

Michael said, "I guess I didn't have much to be thankful for. I always went to Thanksgiving at a restaurant when I was there. I had invites from people in the firm, but I always wanted to be alone. My dad always busted my balls about it."

Diana said, "That is so sad. I agree with your dad." Michael, sitting up in bed and reaching for his jeans on the floor, said, "This year, I have a lot to be thankful for, but it's also bittersweet. My dad loved this holiday. He would get so excited when my mom and I would start planning the menu. He would always go off and do all of the food shopping; he delighted in purchasing everything on the grocery list. He would sneak into the kitchen and sample food all day, like a little kid who couldn't wait to open his presents."

Diana smiled at Michael and said, "He'll be there in spirit." Michael didn't say anything.

Diana dropped Michael off at his mom's house. She went inside briefly to hug Sarah and tell her that she was looking forward to

Thanksgiving. She and Michael kissed. Diana said that they would talk later in the day and left to go to work.

Sarah made a fresh pot of coffee, and they both sat at the kitchen table and had a cup. Sarah asked her son, "How was the flight?"

Michael responded, "Crowded but quiet. I kept thinking that I was coming home after being in exile."

Sarah said, "How did it feel?"

"Wonderful."

Sarah looked at her son and said, "Well, I'm glad that you have decided to move back home. It will be nice to have you here."

Michael said, "Family means a lot more to me now. Hawaii means a lot more to me now. I want both in my life. It took me a while to understand that."

Sarah said, "I want that, too, Honey."

Michael got up from the table to pour himself another cup of coffee and said, "Mom, not to change subjects, but we have some serious Thanksgiving prep to do. We're 24 hours out. We need to clean out the refrigerator and get the bird in the chardonnay citrus brine."

Sarah smiled and said, "I'm so glad that you're here. You always insist on getting the largest turkey you can find, even though I can't lift a heavy turkey anymore."

"That's why I'm here, mom."

Sarah continued, "I wouldn't have done Thanksgiving this year. I didn't have the heart. Thank you for getting me to change my mind."

Michael again said, "That's why I'm here, mom. Okay, what are you going to make?"

Sarah thought about it and said, "I can make the macadamia-nut crunchy pea salad and the maple-glazed sweet potatoes. Diana is bringing the pies."

Michael said, "Okay. I will brine and cook the bird, make the stuffing, make the garlic green beans, the port-orange cranberry sauce, and the thyme Madeira gravy. Janice can make the apple *tarte tatin*. She's good at that. Let's get a list together, and we'll go food shopping. We might need to go to Costco—in fact, we should probably start there."

Sarah said, "Okay, dear. I'll get ready."

CHAPTER 27

Michael drove Sarah's V70 up to the Hawaii Kai Costco, where they were able to get a fresh, organic twenty-five-pound turkey, much to Michael's delight. They bought wine for the brine and for drinking at dinner, a huge bag of fresh cranberries, brown sugar, the ingredients for the stuffing, and enough sweet potatoes to feed a small army. Michael grabbed a few pounds of *poke* for nibbling on. The checkout lines were long. Michael was always amazed at how many procrastinators there were on the day before Thanksgiving.

They drove back home, unloaded all of the food, and headed out to one of the supermarkets in Kailua town, where they grabbed the remaining items on their shopping list. They ate a quick lunch at a Vietnamese café nearby, both ordering lemon grass chicken sandwiches, rolls to share, and two Vietnamese iced coffees.

When they got home, Michael put the turkey in a roasting pan and added the chardonnay, garlic, and citrus brine. He covered the bird with aluminum foil and put the turkey in the refrigerator. He peeled the sweet potatoes and apples, and took two sourdough loaves and made croutons out of them. Typically, he would like the sourdough loaves to sit and harden for a few days before he made the croutons, but he didn't have enough time. So, instead, he baked them at a higher temperature.

When he was finished, he saw his mom sitting out at the kitchen table and staring off at some point in the ocean. Michael came to sit down next to his mom. She turned to him. "I miss your dad more this time of year. This was his favorite holiday."

"Mom, I don't need his favorite holiday to miss him. I miss him all the time. I think about him at least a hundred times a day. I know it is going to be hard without him here, but together, we can get through this."

His mother patted his hands and smiled weakly at him. "You're a good man, Michael. Your father was very proud of you."

"Mom, my dad taught me everything I know."

Michael drove the 280SL to Diana's house in the late afternoon. There were no patients at the base clinic the day before Thanksgiving, so she'd gone home early. She was in her kitchen with the refrigerator door open and bent over when Michael walked in behind her.

"That is some view, sailor."

Diana wiggled her hips in response.

Michael said, "What are you doing down there? It sounds like you're rummaging through your refrigerator like a fucking bear!"

He could hear Diana say, "Turning you on."

Michael said, "Besides that, I thought you don't cook. What are you doing in the fridge?"

Diana stood up and said, "Looking for these." Diana pulled out two bottles of beer and said, "Come on—let's go out to the lanai."

They sat on Diana's lanai, drank beer, and talked.

Michael said, "I can get used to days like this—coming home to my hot fiancée and drinking a beer with her." They clinked bottles.

Diana asked, "How did it go today?"

"We got everything prepped and ready. It'll make tomorrow go a little easier."

Diana took a swig of her beer and said, "How's your mom?"

Michael responded, "She's sad that my dad isn't here, but happy that the rest of the family is around her on Thanksgiving. Even though my dad isn't here, we won't need to remove a chair."

Diana was confused. "What do you mean?"

Michael said, "You. *You're* here. You're going to replace him at the table."

Diana put her beer down and said, "Michael, I will never replace him at the table, but I will gladly borrow his seat for a few hours."

They stripped, left their clothes in a pile in the backyard, and walked over to the hot tub. Michael lit the fire to heat the water and added a couple of logs. They climbed in when the water was still on the cooler side. Diana sat on top of Michael, and he wrapped his arms around her.

Diana said, "I love this."

They went to Kaneohe for dinner at Pahke's and ordered egg drop soup, shrimp *chow fun*, and cashew chicken. They came home and were lying in bed.

Diana said, "I'm very happy. You know that—right?"

Michael said, "I'm glad."

Diana looked into Michael's eyes and said, "If I ever decide to leave you again, please have me committed."

Michael said, playfully, "I thought if you left me, you said that you would shack up with Isaac."

Diana hit him with a pillow.

Michael got up at dawn and threw on a pair of surf trunks that he'd bought a few weeks before. He'd brought them back with him to Atlanta but never took them out of his luggage. He got dressed.

Diana was able to trade her ICU shift with a colleague and was off, but she decided to get up early.

Michael asked her if she wanted to walk the beach. Diana got out of bed, put on a two-piece bikini and low-cut boy shorts, and slathered herself with sunscreen. Michael put on his flip-flops, watch, and a t-shirt, and grabbed his wallet. They took Diana's car down to the beach park. They walked the length of the beach holding hands. Afterwards, they stopped at Starbucks for coffee and fresh oat cakes, and got flowers for Sarah's table. They drove back to Diana's house, where they showered and changed. Diana decided that she wanted to help in the kitchen, or at least observe some of the magic that went on there, and they drove to the Grand house in Diana's car.

Sarah was already busy. She had the Macy's Day Parade on and was assembling the sweet potatoes. She looked up and saw Michael and Diana entering the kitchen and said, "Good morning, kids. Happy Thanksgiving!" They all hugged.

Sarah immediately put Diana to work, and Michael assembled his stuffing. They worked in the kitchen a while longer, and Diana left to go home to change and pick up Janice, whose plane was landing in a few hours. Michael ate some of the *poke* that he'd purchased the day before. He put the bird in the oven and sat on the couch to watch the dog show. Sarah found him sleeping, and she went back to work.

Michael woke up when Janice came in and said, "Hi. Just you?"

Janice said, "Dan didn't want to come, and he made a big deal about the kids coming without him. So, yes—just me." Janice sat down next to her brother on the couch and said, "Michael, you went to law school in Denver. You must have some names of some good divorce attorneys. Can we talk sometime this weekend?"

Michael said, sadly, "Yes. I'm sorry. I'll give you a few good names. I'm glad you're here. It means a lot to mom. Go make your *tarte tatin*."

Janice went to put her luggage in her old bedroom and came out to the kitchen.

Sarah said, happily, "Look who it is! You've joined us at the right time. Diana has been a big help."

Diana hugged Sarah, who was working next to her. Janice got to work on her apple tart.

Sarah watched Janice, Michael, and Diana working together in the kitchen, and the sight made her very happy. She held up a glass of water and said, "To my kids."

CHAPTER 28

Sarah and Diana set the table for eight people. Sarah got out the good dishes. Both commented how great the table looked. Sarah turned off the TV and put on music. She opened the lanai doors and the front windows, and a gentle breeze filled the house. It was starting to look like Thanksgiving would turn out to be a nice day. Sarah remembered that, on one Thanksgiving, a hurricane hit the islands, and she had to have one of the family friends cook the turkey because they had power, and the Grands did not. One Thanksgiving, one of Isaac's friends had convinced him to jump off the roof, and Isaac landed with a thud in the back yard while everyone was eating, breaking both of his ankles. Something odd always seemed to happen on Thanksgiving.

Billy, Kimberly, Jack, and Ryan arrived at 6 PM. Michael had taken the turkey out of the oven and replaced it with the stuffing. He went to go change in his bedroom, and Diana followed him. Janice was drinking a glass of wine in the kitchen and talking to Sarah. Billy and Kimberly walked in, with Jack and Ryan right behind.

Billy said, "Hi, Mrs. Grand. Happy Thanksgiving!"

Sarah said, "Hi, Billy. Kimberly, you look as beautiful as ever." They all hugged.

Jack said, "Hi, Auntie Sarah."

Sarah said, "Hi, boys—you're getting so big!"

Janice came out of the kitchen and hugged Billy and Kimberly. Janice said, "Kimberly, it's been at least 10 years since I've seen you. You haven't aged a day!"

Kimberly said, "Hey, Janice. It's nice to see you!"

Diana and Michael came in a few minutes later. Billy and Michael hugged. Diana hugged Kimberly as Kimberly said, "Congratulations! Let me see the ring!" Kimberly checked it out and said, "Michael, you obviously love this woman."

Michael responded to Kimberly, "Yep. Thanks for noticing."

They milled about while the stuffing cooked. Sarah asked everyone what they wanted to drink. The group went outside with their drinks. It had started to rain, and everyone watched the water start to trickle down from the lanai's roof. Down in the ocean, they saw an intrepid lonely kayaker trying to take advantage of the fact that no one was in the water, getting in some last-minute quality paddle time before the food orgy known as Thanksgiving was to begin.

Michael heard the timer go off for the stuffing and went into the kitchen to pull it out and let it cool. Michael quickly carved up the turkey, which was cooling on the kitchen counter. He came out with a beer and stood next to Billy. They clinked bottle tops.

"Thanks for coming."

"Thanks for inviting."

"Billy, you have an open invite."

The rain was starting to come down harder, and the wind was blowing it into the lanai, so everyone got up and went inside.

Kimberly said, "Smells great in here."

Michael said, "Just wait until you eat it. All the Grands slaved with love to bring you this meal."

Everyone sat down. Sarah put Michael at the head of the table, the spot that used to be reserved for his dad. Michael thought, *Dad was the glue that held this family together. Is this my role now?*

Sarah held up her glass and said, "It's a hard time for me to be thankful for much, but I'm thankful for all of you in my life. You've taught me that we can still live despite absence and loss. It might take time to go forward, but we will always be here together. We can get through this much easier if we lean on each other. Thank you for being here."

Michael read an email that he had received earlier from Isaac. *Dear family, being deployed on Thanksgiving is the loneliest time to be in the Navy. I miss you all. I wish I was there. I will see you in a few months. Love, Isaac.* Michael said that Isaac got to join us. Everyone clapped and started eating. There was music playing in the background, but it didn't didn't dilute the conversation.

Diana must have had three portions of stuffing. She kept going to the stuffing serving dish, which brought on Billy's infectious laugh, and, soon, everyone was laughing.

For a brief moment, Michael looked over at his mom and thought that she looked content. Michael looked over at Diana, and her eyes were sparkling. Michael thought to himself, *For the first time in a long time, I have much to be thankful for.*

The next day, Diana was off and decided to go shopping with Sarah and Janice. Diana picked them up, and they headed off for a girls' day out. Michael said that he might meet them for lunch but asked Diana to text him with the plans.

Michael was going into Honolulu to become a Hawaii resident again, a status he had not held in six years. The rain from the day before had diminished, but the roads were still wet and flooded in some areas. Michael gingerly drove the 280SL over the Pali, and he still managed to hydroplane once or twice but was able to correct without losing control of the car. He wished he had his G63, which was probably in Oakland by now. He parked downtown and ran into the DMV. The line was short. When Michael got up to the teller, she told him that she was sorry about his dad. That was Hawaii—everybody knew everybody. Within an hour, Michael Grand had surrendered his Georgia driver's license, gotten a new Hawaii license, and had registered to vote.

Michael drove to Diamond Head, where he parked and watched the surf. From the road up above, the surfers looked like small toys. Diana texted him and asked if he wanted to join the ladies for lunch at Mariposa. Michael responded that he would be there in 30 minutes. He eased the 280SL out into traffic, drove past Kapiolani Park and through Waikiki, and turned in at Ala Moana Shopping center, where he parked and went upstairs to the restaurant in Neiman Marcus. Sarah, Janice, and Diana were already sitting at a table on the lanai when Michael walked in.

Sarah said, "Hi, dear. We're having a delightful day shopping."

Michael said, "Are all y'all talking about me?"

Diana chimed in and said, "A little."

Michael turned to his sister and asked, "Janice, what did you get?"

Janice responded, "I got a pair of True Religion jeans on sale for me, some stuff for the boys."

Nodding to Diana, Michael said, "What did you get?"

Diana winked at him and said, "I'm not telling."

Michael told her, "Just remember—I like Hermès ties."

Diana said, "I'm not saying anything. What I am getting?"

Michael responded, "A ring." Diana feigned dismay and said, "*That's it?*"

Michael said, "Yep."

Sarah giggled.

Diana said, "I'm not telling you what I got you, either, Michael."

Michael said, "I don't need anything. I already got the best gift this year."

Diana was beaming. Sarah was smiling wildly.

Michael pulled out his wallet, took out his Hawaii driver's license, and said, "It's official."

Sarah, Janice, and Diana clapped.

Michael said, "I think I want to stay a while longer this time."

They all finished their lunch and talked for a bit. Diana, Sarah, and Janice still had some more shopping to do, and Michael said that he had to run an errand.

After he left his family, Michael went across the street to the Ala Moana Yacht Club and met a buddy from high school who had a Tahitian pearl business. He bought Diana a strand of flawless graduated black pearls; she'd always loved Tahitian pearls but had never got around to buying them for herself.

CHAPTER 29

Diana and Michael went over to Sarah's for leftovers. Then they went home, opened a bottle of wine, sat outside on the lanai and listened to Jimmy Smith's *Back at the Chicken Shack* playing on the stereo in the living room through the open doors. By Hawaii standards, it was a chilly night, and Diana went in to get a quilt to wrap herself with. After a while, Michael wanted some of the quilt, and he wrapped it around both of them. They snuggled together in the cool November evening.

Diana said, "Nice moment."

Michael said, "Sure is."

Diana continued, "I guess we should start talking about the wedding."

Michael asked, "What do you want—big or small?"

Diana, who grew up as an only child and had a few close friends but not a lot of friends, said, without hesitation, "Small."

Michael said, "Hotel or beach?"

Diana didn't need even a second to respond. "Beach."

Michael said, "Sunrise or sunset?"

Diana said, "Sunset."

Michael said, "Hawaiian music or DJ?"

Diana said, "Both."

Michael said, "When?"

Diana asked Michael, "When does Isaac come back?"

Michael said, "June."

Diana smiled and said, "I've always wanted to be a June bride."

Michael responded, "I always thought that, if I ever got married, I would want my dad to marry us. I guess that's not going to happen."

Diana was running her hands through Michael's curly hair. "What about getting a judge he worked with? That would be kind of cool. It's like he would be there in spirit."

Michael thought about it for a minute and said, "Hmm. I'll have to see what I can do."

Michael said, "I'm getting married for the first time when I am 45. Is that *weird*?"

Diana responded, "I'm 45, too. How is that weird?"

Michael said, "I don't know. My parents married when my mom was twenty-two and my dad was twenty-five. Most people get married earlier than age 45."

Diana said, "As long as we found each other, who cares?"

Michael said, "We found each other a long time ago. Why didn't we do this sooner?"

Diana sighed and said, "Standard excuses. I wasn't ready. You weren't ready. Medical school. Law school."

Michael interrupted. "*The proctologist.*"

Diana said to no one in particular, "Him."

Michael said, "Think about it. We could have been married for more than 25 years at this point."

Diana climbed on top of Michael and said, "That's not the way the universe works, Michael."

Michael thought about Diana's answer and said, "We really found each other when the universe told us that we were ready."

Diana said, "That is very Zen of you, Michael."

Michael looked into Diana's eyes and said, "It's true, Diana."

Diana said, "It is. I'm just glad that I rediscovered you at all."

Michael concurred. "Me, too. Just wait until you see what you're getting for Hanukkah."

Diana started tickling Michael and said, "I thought I was only getting a ring."

Michael threw Diana off of him and rolled on top of her. "You'll see."

"All I want is you, Michael."

Michael said, "You have that—it's a given. You're getting something else, too. It's cool—I promise."

Diana said, "Can I have a hint?"

Michael replied, "Nope."

A few seconds later, she asked, "A new car?"

Michael said, "Uh, no. That's something you buy yourself."

Diana continued, "A puppy?"

Michael yawned and said, "I'm not telling."

Diana finally said, "Jewelry. You are getting me more jewelry."

Michael said, "I just spent 20 grand on some jewelry for you."

Diana, shocked, said, "Oh, *fuck*. Was the ring really that *much*?" Despite being a physician and Navy Captain, Diana had never forgotten her middle-class upbringing and never really spent money on herself.

Michael kissed Diana and said, "Do you like it?"

Diana said, "No—I *love* it."

Michael smiled and said, "Then it was worth every penny."

Diana looked up to the ceiling and said, loudly, "I love this man!"

Michael said, "Right back at you, kid."

Michael and Diana woke up with the doves right after sunrise.

Michael said, "Come on. Let's go walk the beach. I need to exercise after all that food we've eaten during the past few days."

Diana giggled and said, "I think we should do indoor exercise. Doctor's orders."

Michael, feigning surprise, asked, "What do you prescribe, Doctor?"

Diana winked and said, "I'll show you."

Afterwards, they still walked the beach.

Michael said, "I never get tired of this beach."

Diana responded, "This is why we live here and put up with the high cost of living, the congestion, and the stress. It's for this beach."

Michael said, "True. At some point, I'll have to get a job, and I won't be able to walk Kailua Beach every day, but until then, I'll walk it as much as I can."

Diana asked, "Have you heard from Marvin?"

Michael said, "Nope. If this is meant to be, this will happen."

Diana asked, "What will you do if it doesn't happen?"

Michael said, "I don't know. I'll figure something out. I can always get my old job back. I just don't know if I want to do trial work anymore."

Diana responded, "Michael, you have worked since you were 18 years old. You work like your father worked. Work defines you. You need to do something."

Michael said, "I will. Trust me. But it's kind of nice to take a little break."

CHAPTER 30

Michael drove to Ala Moana shopping center to get some dress slacks and to start shopping for some Hanukkah gifts for his family. When he drove up, he saw all of the Christmas decorations, including the giant Santa Claus wearing shorts and an aloha shirt, sitting with his legs in front of him, smiling a big Hawaiian smile with one hand giving a *shaka* sign. Michael walked into the men's section of Neiman Marcus, looked at the various racks, and selected a few pairs of pants.

Then he walked to the large table containing all the ties. He always bought ties for his dad for Hanukkah. He immediately found two that he liked and another that he thought that his dad would like, grabbing all three before he realized what he was doing. He started to walk back to the table and return the ties that he'd selected, but then he decided to still purchase them for himself. Michael ate lunch alone, thinking about his dad and how he missed him.

Michael drove home and went over to his mom's house. Janice was sitting out on the lanai, listening to her iPod. Michael and Janice had that in common—they both loved their music.

Michael asked his sister, "What are you listening to?"

"Jay-Z."

Michael sat down next to his sister. "I saw him once, going up the escalator at the Lennox Square Neiman's. I was going down, and he was going up with a whole entourage of people behind him. He had a big smile on his face, and he was talking to someone on his left. Kind of a cool moment." He sat down next to Janice and said, "What's going on with you? You mentioned something about divorce lawyers."

Janice turned off her iPod and took her ear buds out of her ears. "It looks like it's heading in that direction. Dan has talked to some attorneys."

Michael asked, "Do you remember their names?

Janice thought about it and said, "Mike somebody. Last name begins with an H."

Michael said, "*Halston*? Mike Halston?"

Janice nodded and said, "Yes, that's him."

"Janice, Mike Halston is a big dog. He's an $800-an-hour divorce lawyer. He's really good at what he does. In law school, he was always an asshole. In first year, he would hide the case books that we all needed so that he could find the answers to exam questions and the rest of us couldn't. One of my buddies slashed his tires."

Janice sighed.

Michael continued, "I have some names, and they're great lawyers. You need a great lawyer against Mike Halston. Are you sure this is what you want to do?"

Janice continued, "I haven't been happy in a while."

Her brother continued, "Is this what Dan wants?"

"I don't know. He mentioned that he met with the lawyers and that he doesn't want to upset the kids. He's not around much."

"Janice, the last time I checked, divorce requires two parties. Have you tried therapy?"

Janice said, "Yes, but nothing really happened. Dan went initially but then stopped going altogether. It's like he's already given up."

Michael put his arm around his sister. "Well, just because he's talking to Mike Halston doesn't mean that he's looking for a divorce. He's going to get hammered. He makes way more than you."

Janice interrupted her brother. "I do okay."

Michael continued, "I'm not saying you don't, but he makes more than you, and the law is pretty simple with regard to one spouse who makes more than the other."

Janice, staring out at the ocean, said, "Maybe I'll just move here with the kids."

Michael said, "Somehow, I think that Dan will contest that decision. Do you think there's someone else?"

Janice looked at her brother and said, "What—that he's *seeing* someone?

Michael said, "Yes."

"I don't know. I never really thought that he was the type, but I don't know. He's always working. I don't think he'd have the time."

Michael, always the counselor, said, "I've never really had much faith in people who want to end their marriage, but if it gets to the irreconcilable-differences point, divorce is a good tool to end it when two people want to end it. Trust me, I've seen lots of couples get divorced, and I can tell when both parties want to call their marriage. Call me naïve, but I don't see it with you. I don't think that you're there yet."

Janice started to tear up.

Michael continued, "I still think you should call a few names on the list that I give you, just to protect your ass, but I think you should wait and see if Dan goes through with it."

Janice leaned in toward her brother and put her head on his shoulder. "Thanks for the talk."

Michael said, "Always. I'll come by later and take you to the airport."

Janice said, "Oh, awesome. I would have taken a cab."

Michael got up and kissed Janice on the forehead.

He went home, and he and Diana went out to dinner and to an early movie. Then Michael took his sister to the airport and watched from the departures drop-off area as she disappeared into the throng of post-Thanksgiving travelers.

CHAPTER 31

Diana got up at 5 AM. She threw on workout clothes
for a quick gym session before she had to be at Tripler
by 7:30. She kissed Michael, who was still in bed, watching the
morning news.

Michael said to her, pointing at the TV, "*Did you see this?* There's
a tropical storm that's 1500 miles off the coast of the Big Island.
Moving at 26 mph."

Diana, in a hurry, seemed to brush off Michael's concern. "It's
that time of year. There's always a storm out there. I have to go. Let's
eat in tonight."

Michael said, "Not a problem. I'll take care of dinner."

Diana grabbed her bags and said, "Bye. Have a good day."

"Bye. You, too. Love you."

Diana was already out of the house and didn't hear Michael's
response.

Michael threw on a pair of surf trunks, his watch, a t-shirt, a hat,
and sunglasses and went to his mom's house to see if she wanted to
go walk the beach.

Sarah was already dressed and was getting ready to leave. "Hi, Honey."

Michael said, "Hi, mom. Want to walk the beach?"

Sarah said, "You go ahead. I have to be at Queen's by ten. I'm meeting with some people from the ER. Seems like my old job opened up, and they might want me to come back full time. They said they would make it worth my while."

Michael said, "Mom, do you want to be Unit Director again of one of the busiest ERs between San Francisco and Tokyo?"

Sarah said, "I think there are some benefits." Sarah kissed Michael on the cheek. "Bye, Honey. Have a good day."

Michael said, "You, too. Good luck!"

Michael walked the beach by himself. The ocean was calm and looked like green glass. There were a few kite surfers out on the water, taking advantage of a decent offshore wind. A catamaran was heading out to Flat Island. Overhead, a Navy SH-60 Seahawk was heading toward the Marine Corps Base, the only obstruction in an otherwise clear blue sky. It was on days like this that Michael felt he was very lucky to live in Hawaii. He stopped off at Starbucks for coffee. When he came out, he saw Billy standing outside.

Billy said, "I saw the car. I figured you were in that bourgeois excuse for really bad coffee."

Michael said, "Have a minute? I'll buy you a cup."

Billy said, "Deal."

They went back in, and Billy got a Venti Thai Latte. They sat outside. Billy turned down the volume on his radio.

Michael said, "How are you?"

Billy said, between sips, "Good. How are you?"

Michael continued, "Good. Hey, Bill. My car should be arriving next week. Do I have to get it safety inspected?"

Billy said, "Yep. Within 30 days. You have to register it, too."

Michael said, "Thanks. That's what I thought. I'll do all of that on the same day. There's still a DMV in Kaneohe—right? Near the courthouse?"

Billy nodded and said, "Yep, not far."

Michael told his friend, "Cool. I went down to the location on Fort Street on Friday, and the clerk told me that she was sorry about my dad. I figure I can go to the DMV in Kaneohe and no one will know me."

Billy chuckled. "Mike, you were a pretty well-known trial lawyer here for many years before you abruptly moved away because some broad broke your heart. Everyone here knows you."

Michael had to think about that one for a minute. He always thought that he was working in his dad's shadow. He didn't really realize that maybe he had his own identity, independent of his dad's. He said, "Hey, let's take the *Res Ipsa* out this weekend."

Billy stood up and said, "I would love to, if we don't have a hurricane coming."

Michael stood up, too. "I was talking about that with Diana this morning. She seemed to minimize it."

Billy shook his head and said, "What does she know?"

Michael said, "She's in the Navy. Maybe she has access to secret weather shit."

Billy looked at his friend and said, "Michael, how many hurricanes have you been in?

Michael responded, "Two. *Iwa* and *Iniki*."

Billy continued, "And during those two hurricanes, do you remember how the weather was before the hurricanes hit?"

Michael thought for a second and said, "Perfect—just like today. I even told myself how awesome it was today when I walked the beach."

Billy said, *"Perfect—just like today."*

Michael said, "Are you worried?"

"Mike, I don't ever worry until bad news is in my hand."

Michael said, "Yeah. Me, too."

Billy said, "I know. That's why I love you. I have to go." They fist-bumped.

CHAPTER 32

Sarah was offered the ER Unit Director job, her old job, at the Queen's Medical Center. She accepted. She didn't need to work because of money, but she had to work because sitting around the house with recurrent thoughts about Joshua and how difficult it was to live without him all the time wasn't healthy. It wasn't that she was moving on. She wasn't, but she was ready to move Joshua to a smaller place in her heart rather than assign him her entire heart, as she had done when he was alive. Sarah told HR that she would start the next day. She called Michael from the car to tell him.

Michael said, "Wow! That's great news. You loved your job there."

Sarah said, "I did."

Her son continued, "So, you want to go back to the rat race?"

His mom said, "Michael, I never got tired of it. I quit when your dad got sick to care for him. We were supposed to both retire in two years and start traveling more, visit the kids in their various locations. Your dad would tell me that I should be working instead of being with a sick old man. I told him it was a great privilege to care for him. Now, I have to think about me. I still have a few years left to contribute. I want to go back. I think it will do me some good."

Michael said, "I'm very proud of you, mom. You don't have dad anymore, but you have me and Diana."

Sarah said, "Thank you, Honey. That's very special."

Michael stopped at the supermarket and looked at what fresh fish was in. He wasn't liking anything in the case, so he bought two live Maine Lobsters, a pound of clams, a pound of scallops, a pound of fresh prawns, corn on the cob, fish stock, a package of bay leaves, some hot sauce, and the best bottle of pinot noir he could find. Then he went to Target and bought the largest and cheapest stockpot they had available. Tonight, he and Diana would have an old-fashioned East Coast clambake, the kind they would enjoy when they spent weekends together in college.

Diana came home around 6 PM and said, "Wow! That smells good."

Michael opened the pot and let her look in.

She said, "Wow! That *looks* good." They kissed.

Michael asked her, "How was your day?"

Diana said, "Hectic."

Michael held out a glass of the pinot noir and said, "Want a glass of wine?"

Diana said, "Yes. Let me change first."

Diana came out about 15 minutes later, wearing jeans and a GORUCK t-shirt. Michael had assembled the meal outside, and they ate on the lanai. The light wind was pushing around the palm fronds high up in the palm trees.

Michael asked his fiancée, "Why was your day hectic?"

Diana said, "Administrative stuff. All kinds of meetings. Meetings with the Hospital Command Staff. Meetings about medical-airlift-command readiness. Meetings about mass-casualty training. And there were 40 patients at Sick Call today. We had to bring in a corpsman and a nurse to help triage all the patients."

Michael said, "Sounds hectic."

Diana drank a sip of her pinot noir and said to Michael, "What did you do today?"

Michael said, "Not much. My mom took the ER Unit Director job at Queen's. She's starting tomorrow."

Diana said, between sips of wine, "If that's what she wants to do, I'm supportive. That's a stressful job. Does she want to go back so soon after your dad died?"

Michael nodded, "She doesn't need to work—my dad took care of that. But I think that she's looking at it more like a distraction and thinks that she's not quite ready to retire yet."

Diana said, "Well, I can certainly understand throwing yourself into work as a distraction."

Michael looked into his wine glass and said, "Me, too. It was my mantra for the past six years. In my time in Atlanta, I had two relationships, and both ended badly. I threw myself into work. Billy met one of them when he and Kimberly visited. I was able to use the law-firm corporate box for a Falcons game, and we all went. She was a drug rep. I could tell Billy didn't like her; he's very perceptive."

Diana said, "That's pretty much how I was, too. There was Doug, but that was it."

Michael giggled and said, *"Was that the proctologist's name?"*

Diana said, quietly, "Yes."

Michael took another sip of his wine, and he said, "Huh—I never knew his name."

Diana looked at him, a little annoyed, and said, "Is it important?"

Michael responded, "No—not at all. I hope he's happy and has found true love. I'm glad he passed on you."

Diana said, "Actually, I passed on him. He asked me to marry him about four years ago. Initially, I said 'Yes.' Then my dad got sick, and, when he died, I woke up one day and realized I wasn't in love with him. I gave him the ring back. I heard that he became Chief of Urology at Bethesda, made Captain, is married. I, too, hope he's happy."

Michael looked at Diana and asked, "Are you happy?"

Diana said, "I am happy. For the first time in a long time, I can say that."

Michael grabbed his wine glass and toasted Diana. He said, "Thank you for rescuing me. If I hadn't found you, I don't think I would have wound up a very happy man. I think I would have been that guy who died at his desk."

Diana looked Michael in the eyes and said, "I've never been happier than when I've been with you. I am looking forward to spending the rest of my life with you." They kissed. Diana said, "So, does Billy like me?"

Michael looked at Diana. "No, sweetheart—Billy *loves* you."

CHAPTER 33

Michael and Diana awoke to the alarm at 6:30 AM. Michael went out to the lanai and looked out. The sky was bright red, just like the old warning he learned as a teenager. *Red skies at morning, sailors take warning.* Michael paid attention to the ominous-looking skies.

Diana turned on the news on the TV in the bedroom. Overnight, the Central Pacific Hurricane Center had upgraded tropical storm TS-13 to Hurricane *Moke*, with maximum sustained winds of 105 mph. Hurricane *Moke* was approximately 950 miles southwest of the Big Island.

Michael was looking at a satellite image of the hurricane. He said, "*Fuck*—that is a well-defined storm."

Just then, Diana's pager went off, and her cell phone rang simultaneously. She went into another room to take the call. Michael could hear her talking, but it was muffled through the door. She was walking back into the bedroom, and she was still on the phone. Diana said, "Yes, sir. I'll be there." Diana hung up the phone. She stripped and got into the shower. Diana continued, "I have to get out of here. Tripler has just implemented its Hospital Incident Command System. I have to report in. I don't know how long this is going to take, but I think I'll be up there for a while." Diana got dressed, kissed Michael, and left.

Michael called his mom. She answered while she was driving to her first day of work. Michael said, "Hi, mom. I hear that there is a little hurricane coming. I was just talking with Diana, and she said that Tripler had just instituted its incident command system."

Sarah was all business. "Mike, Queen's just did the same thing. They called me in early to get things going. They are preparing for a mass-casualty situation."

Michael said, "Shit. Can you check in with me later, let me know how things are going?"

Sarah said, "Yes, if I can. I have to go. I'm pulling into the parking lot now."

Michael said, "Hell of a first day back."

His mom actually managed a little laugh. Sarah said, "They told me in the interview yesterday that they would love to have me back and that they would promise that I wouldn't be bored."

Michael said, "Looks like they were right."

He jumped into the shower but heard his phone ringing. He ran out to the bedroom naked and with shampoo in his eyes, which was starting to sting. It was a number he didn't recognize. "Hello?"

The voice on the other end said, "Hi, this is Alii Towing. The shipper has given us your 2011 G63 because they don't want it sitting on the dock when a hurricane comes in. Can we bring it to you in about two hours?" Michael told them they could and gave him the address of his mom's house, instead of Diana's.

Michael walked down to the beach. The day was beginning as a splendid tropical morning—calm, with a moderate breeze. He saw other residents of beach homes begin to move their sailboats from the sand and up to their property lines. Some were shuttering their windows. Michael went into the garage and found the old portable generator and moved it outside of the house to the front lanai. He retrieved a cordless drill and hammer from his dad's workbench and brought them into the house. Michael secured the storm shutters on the windows facing the ocean. The original owner had them installed, and they had been well used over the years.

A half-hour later, a flatbed pulled into the driveway; his car was sitting on the bed. The driver said to Michael, "I like your truck." Mike said, "Thanks. It's a fun toy." He stared at his G63 for a minute. He truly loved this car. He signed the manifest, and the driver lowered the car. Michael tipped the guy $40 and told him to stay safe. The driver told Michael the same thing.

Michael measured the dimensions of the windows on the front of the house, went over to Diana's, and repeated the exercise. Michael drove to Ace Hardware and had them cut plywood in the shapes and sizes of all the windows. Ace was jammed with people wanting to do whatever they could to secure their homes from the incoming storm. Michael purchased a cheap moving blanket, batteries, deck screws, candles, and rope. One of the employees came over to the car with a forklift, and they placed the plywood sheets on the roof and tied them down with the rope.

Michael then drove to the supermarket. It was also packed with people trying to get supplies before the storm arrived. Although the store was half empty of products, he was able to purchase four cases of water and some canned food. Michael drove home and placed the plywood sheets on all the windows that weren't already secured with shutters. It was hard work for only one person, and it took Michael several hours to complete the task. He was sweating and sore by the time he finished.

Then he drove to Diana's and repeated the task.

It was late afternoon by the time he gingerly climbed back into his G63 and drove home. He went in and took a nap with the TV on. Hurricane *Moke* was now 300 miles away. The winds were starting to pick up. Michael drove to his mom's house and parked the G63 on the side of the house by the beach-access path. He made sure that it was not under any trees.

Sarah called and said, "Hi, Mike. They're evacuating Kailua to the various area high schools. I think you should go to one of the evacuation centers."

Michael said, "Mom, this house is made out of lava rock, and it's survived many hurricanes. I think I'll be okay."

Sarah was insistent, "Michael, they are predicting that the storm will be a direct hit on the islands. I think you should evacuate."

Michael told his mom, "Mom, I'll be fine. I went to Ace and bought plywood boards to put up on the windows. I bought water. There is plenty of canned food in the pantry. I pulled out the generator. I have candles. I have the fireplace. I have firearms. I will be safest here. We've done this before."

Sarah sighed and said, "Okay. I guess I can't argue with you."

Michael said, "At least I know that all the people I love will be surrounded by several feet of concrete." Both Queen's and Tripler were designed to take much worse. "Mom, I'll be fine. If it gets crazy and I can safely evacuate, I will. I promise."

Sarah said, "Michael. Be safe. I will try to be in contact if I can. Love you."

Michael said, "Love you, mom. Be safe."

Just as soon as Sarah ended the call, Diana called.

Michael said, "Hi. How's it going?" Michael could tell from Diana's voice that she was stressed.

She said, "Busy here. The Army and Navy know what to do when there is a crisis. It's organized chaos. We are basically on war footing. Everyone has a job and a responsibility. Some Navy ships out at sea have started to evacuate their patients to us."

CHAPTER 34

Tripler Army Medical Center, built in 1907, housed the Pacific Regional Medical Command and was central to the war efforts of every conflict since the First World War. Massive, and painted pink, it is a very identifiable landmark. Its pink color has always been subject to urban mythology. Some believed that the pink color was designed to confuse the Japanese into thinking that it was the Royal Hawaiian Hotel in Waikiki so they would not attack it. The Royal Hawaiian was the exact same shade of pink. Others believed that it was pink and not hospital white because it matched the color of the red dirt in the Moanalua area, where Tripler was built. The wind would constantly blow the dirt around, and the Army Corps of Engineers didn't want to keep painting it white. Tripler is a modern tertiary-care center and one of the largest in the Pacific Basin.

Diana said, "Hurricanes are no fun."

Michael asked, "Is this your first?"

Diana responded, "Yes."

"Diana, you're going to be safe up there, Tripler could probably survive a direct bomb attack. No hurricane will touch you."

Diana said, "I see that they are evacuating low-lying areas, including Kailua. Are you going to evacuate?"

Michael said, "Nah. As I told my mom, the Grand house is made out of lava. I have a generator, a fireplace, water, food, firearms if the zombies try to come in and eat my ass. I boarded up the windows. I did that at your place, too, by the way."

Diana seemed a bit more at ease and said, "Oh, thank you. I was worried about that."

Michael said, "I'm going to ride it out, here. This old house has been down this road before. It knows what to do."

Diana couldn't argue with her stubborn fiancé. "Well, you be safe out there. I wish I was there with you. Sounds kind of like fun."

Michael said, "You, too. Talk or text when you can." Michael could sense that Diana was nervous that he was staying in the house. "Baby, I'll be fine."

Diana said, "Okay. Love you."

Michael said, "Love you" and hung up the phone.

The phone rang again. It was Billy.

Michael answered the phone by saying, "Fuck, the phone has been ringing off the hook."

Billy said, "You know they're evacuating Kailua—right?"

Michael said, "And what? I'm going to put a blanket down at Kailua High School with hundreds of other people? The roof can blow off from there, too."

Billy said, "I know. Just be safe down there. This is going to be a huge fucking storm. We're probably going to lose power and communications, but I'll try to check in with you. See you when this is all over."

"Be safe out there, Bill."

Billy said, "Kimberly and the kids are with her parents in Kaimuki. At least they're up on a hill."

Michael said, "This is a tough little house, Bill. It'll survive; it has before. If you get stuck, come over. I have a generator and plenty of food and water."

Billy said, "If I'm not needed, I'll come over."

Michael responded, "Be safe."

"You, too."

The winds started to pick up. Michael could hear the surf becoming angry and see the trees sway. He went out to check the generator. He tested it, and it worked fine. Michael looked toward the driveway. Some debris had already started to accumulate in the front yard. It was raining hard, and water had begun to pool around the big mango tree. He had the TV on. The hurricane had begun to downgrade as it hit the Big Island, but the maximum sustained winds were still at 90 mph. Michael could hear the rain hitting the shutters and the plywood boards. It was now moving down the island chain and was pummeling the island of Kauai. As it moved from island to island, it began losing steam. The newscaster said that when it hit Oahu, maximum sustained winds would be 65 mph.

Still enough to kill you, Michael thought.

At 8 PM, he heard a loud bang that sounded like a bomb going off, and the power immediately went out. It was the neighborhood transformer. Michael went outside to the generator, sitting on the front lanai. The wind was howling, and rain was coming in under the roof of the lanai and was hitting Michael straight in the face. Years ago, Joshua had installed an inlet receptacle near the front of the house to be able to connect up to the generator. Michael connected up the cabling and fired up the generator; the power to the house came back on. It was nice to have power during a hurricane.

Michael walked back into the house. The rear shutters were rattling loudly in the face of the wind, but all of them had managed to stay closed. It sounded like the roof was about to tear off the house and fly into the air, but so far, it was staying put.

CHAPTER 35

For the next four hours, the wind and rain were unrelenting. Michael would hear loud crashes and glass shatter. He also heard loud pops as other transformers would blow. Michael thought it would be fun to truly experience what the storm felt like. He put on his old North Face jacket and opened the rear lanai door. It felt like the wind was pushing against the house, and Michael could barely open the door. Michael stepped outside. The wind sounded like the freight trains that he would hear when he drove to his office in Atlanta. The wind was whipping the rain directly into Michael's face, and his eyes stung from the impact. Michael turned back around and ran inside, making sure that the sliding door was secure and that no water was leaking into the house. At one point, a coconut flew into one of the plywood boards, and Michael heard a loud crack.

Around 11 PM, it got eerily quiet. The wind almost stopped. It was still raining. The eye was passing overhead. Michael went outside to check the generator; its diesel engine was still chugging along. He saw lights pull up the driveway. It was Billy, in his F-150.

Billy got out, wearing a long yellow raincoat. He said, "I figured this house was still standing. Plus, you have power. The station is on reserve power. It's a mess out there; a lot of roads have flooded. There is tons of debris and shit on the road. I drove by Diana's house before I came here. It looks like part of her roof blew off."

Michael said, "Fuck. Buddy, come inside."

They both got in, out of the rain. Michael said to Billy, "Give me that jacket. You look like a fucking U-Boat captain."

Michael put Billy's wet jacket on the kitchen table, next to his jacket that he'd used a few hours earlier.

Billy said, "The storm should start back up in a few minutes, when the eye leaves the area. For the most part, it looks like Oahu dodged the worst of it. The Big Island, Maui, and Kauai got pounded. They are reporting huge amounts of damage and a few casualties."

Michael said, "I have food, beer, and TV. We can have a little party."

Billy said, "See the uniform? I'm still on duty. If there's a need, I have to head out. But, hopefully I won't get called, it will be nice and quiet, and we can escape the storm outside in this house." They sat down on the couch and watched the TV that was turned to the news.

Michael asked, "How much damage was there to Diana's house?"

Billy said, "Aside from the roof, I couldn't tell. It's pretty dark out there—all the street lights are out. But rain was pouring in."

Michael said, "I'll wait to tell her until the morning. She has enough stress right now."

Billy said, "Probably a busy night for them."

As soon as the eye passed over, the full force of the winds picked up again, although both Michael and Billy thought it sounded a lot less intense than when the storm had come in hours earlier. By 1 AM, Hurricane *Moke* had passed over Oahu and had begun to veer out to sea. It was still raining hard, but the winds had died down.

Billy got up and went into the kitchen to grab his raincoat. He said, "I'm going to check in at the station, head over to Kimberly's parents' house, and go spend the night with my family. Thanks for giving me shelter." He and Michael hugged.

Michael said, "Let's check in later, if you are not busy. I think I'll be up on Diana's roof with a tarp."

Michael went to bed shortly after Billy left, and he slept through until dawn. Michael changed into surf trunks and borrowed his dad's Patagonia windbreaker. It was still raining when he went outside. He checked on the G63 and discovered that there was sand all the way up to the hubs, but it looked like it was in pretty good shape. There was a palm frond on the hood, which he removed. A neighbor's Hobie Cat had wound up in the Grands' backyard, upside down, the mast stuck in the sand. There were palm fronds, leaves, and mangoes everywhere.

Michael walked down to the beach. There was a dead hammerhead shark floating in the surf, and debris was strewn up and down the beach, including downed palm trees. There was a mass of fishnets that resembled a large, dead animal and part of someone's roof. Michael walked back up to the house and did a walk-around inspection of the house. The little house had survived another hurricane. He could not find any damage. Sand had completely buried the rear lanai, and two of the Adirondack chairs had flipped over; Michael had forgotten to move them inside. They could easily have become missiles in the storm.

He walked to the front of the house and noticed for the first time that one of the plywood boards he'd nailed up earlier had completely shattered in the middle. The coconut had hit the plywood with the force of a bullet, and the plywood had taken the full impact; the window underneath was fine. *Well, if the only damage was a piece of broken plywood, I can live with that.*

Michael was struck by what the speed of the water and the pounding surf had done to the beach. The beach was used to a nice, slow-and-steady motion of waves rolling in and waves rolling out. The beach could handle this. When the hurricane came in and the speed of the water increased, it rearranged the sand into something that overwhelmed the beach, forcing it to change and redesign. Parts of the beach were washed away completely. Other parts of the beach had been compensated with an abundance of sand. The beach was altered after a storm—irrevocably changed in some areas, renewed in others, but never quite the same as it once was. It dawned on Michael that the Grands of late were like the beach.

Michael climbed into the G63 and pushed the start button. The hand-built 6.3-liter engine growled to life. Michael engaged and locked the three independent differentials, put the car into a crawl, and slowly tried to back out of the sand. The G63 was rocking gently back and forth as it tried to extricate itself from the deep mounds of sand, only to have the tires catch traction. He backed out into the grass in the front of the house. *Man, I love this car,* Michael thought. Michael pulled out of the driveway, turned right, and headed toward Diana's house.

There was still no power in Kailua. The roads were severely flooded, with the water flowing through a canal that bisected Kailua, to the sea and overflowing onto a bridge, washing out the road and making travel dangerous. Michael drove very slowly over the bridge; the water was almost up to the middle of the rims. Nobody was outside. There was debris from houses and palm fronds everywhere. Some large trees had toppled during the night, the rain and wind too much for their root systems. Some houses were damaged. He looked in at one house along the road and saw that a sinkhole had opened in their front yard, swallowing what looked to be a Jetta and a Pathfinder.

The access roads leading to beach homes were covered in sand and leaves. Sand from the beach-access ways had washed up onto the road in clumpy patches, making the road uneven in some areas. Occasionally, Michael would see a stray dog walking alongside the road. Michael wanted to stop, but what could he have done? He pulled into Diana's driveway. Most of the roof had caved in. There were roof shingles all over her front lawn. Sometime during the night, her large black trashcan had become airborne and had smashed through one of her front windows, which allowed rain and debris to flow into the house. One of the big palm trees in her front yard had been blown onto the roof, collapsing a support wall. *Well, I guess that's how the roof caved in*, thought Michael.

He got out of the truck, went to the front window, and peered in. The roof had completely collapsed into the living room. *Good thing we weren't sleeping here last night.* Diana's neighbors were a little luckier—only the house across the street had a destroyed garage. Michael called Diana but didn't think that she would answer. She answered almost immediately and sounded sleepy.

Quietly, Diana answered. "Hello?"

Michael said, "Hi, baby. It's me."

Diana became more alert. "Michael, you're alive!"

Michael felt bad about waking her up and said, "Sorry. Were you sleeping?"

Diana said, "I was up more than 36 hours. I found an empty cot and went down for a little nap."

Michael said, "Was it busy last night?"

Diana responded, "Yes."

Michael continued, "Okay, the good news is that I am alive. The bad news is that one of the palm trees in your front yard fell, blew into your roof, and collapsed it into the living room." Michael could hear that Diana had started crying. Michael told her, "*Hey, hey. It's okay. It's just a thing. We can rebuild. We're alive.*" Michael could tell that Diana was overwhelmed by the news.

She said, "I'm coming home. I want to see it."

Michael continued, "Diana, Honey, the roads are flooded, and power is still out. I want you staying put for a while."

Diana started to cry and said through the tears, "Michael, I'm coming home."

Michael said, "Well, can you see if a nice soldier with a Humvee will take you home? The roads are shit out there."

Diana said, more forcefully, "I'm coming home."

Michael sighed and said, "Hang on. Let me come get you. My car can take it. Seriously—let me come get you. I can be there in probably two hours. I don't know if the freeways are closed, and I might have to go through Kaneohe and up Kunia Road. Let me come get you."

Diana said, "Okay."

Michael said, "I'm leaving now. I'll call you when I pull up in front of Tripler."

CHAPTER 36

Much to Michael's surprise, the freeways were open, and, aside from lots of water, they were relatively free of debris. From his vantage point on the freeway, Michael could see the damage to the island. The lights were off in the tunnel, and when he crossed over to the Honolulu side of the island, Michael got a good look at tall buildings in the downtown and Waikiki. It was eerie. Almost all of the lights were off. The whole island was without power. Michael had rarely seen this before.

There were few people on the road—mostly emergency vehicles—and Michael made it to Tripler in a little less than an hour. He called Diana. Diana answered. He saw what looked like a roadblock manned by soldiers from Schofield Barracks, who were dressed in full battle uniforms and had parked two Humvees by the main entrance to Tripler. Michael said, "Is the US Army going to fucking shoot me if I proceed through the roadblock?"

Diana said, "They might. Hang on. Let me walk down there. What are you driving?"

Michael said, "My car."

Diana said, "*What car*? I don't see your dad's convertible."

Michael said, "I'm not driving the SL. I'm driving a black G63 Mercedes. I'll drive slowly and stop in front of the Army guys."

Diana said, "Hang on. I'll be out in a minute."

Michael left the engine running. He saw Diana come out of the main entrance. She was wearing fatigues, which were soaked. Michael could tell that she was tired. She walked up to the truck, opened the passenger-side door and climbed in. Diana looked at him and said, "*This* is your car? This douche-bag monster?"

Michael said, "Hey, I came here to rescue you, and you're making fun of my car?"

Diana rolled her eyes and said, "This isn't a car. This thing is reserved for asshole oligarchs and rich dudes who have to overcompensate for having a small penis."

Michael said, "Which am I?"

Diana responded, "Neither."

Michael leaned over, kissed Diana, and said, "Well, I'm glad that you have your sense of humor back in light of the bad news I told you earlier. And besides, once I let you drive this car, you will not want to drive anything else."

Diana sat back in the passenger seat, buckled her seatbelt, and said, "Take me home. I want to see my house."

Michael followed the path back to Kailua the way he came. Diana had a pensive look on her face and didn't feel like talking much, so Michael turned on the radio, which was connected into his iPod, and let it randomly shuffle music. By the time they made it back to Kailua, most of the intersections were manned by HPD officers, who'd set up flares on the road to signal that the traffic lights were still off. There was light traffic on the road. Some people were already out collecting the debris and putting it into piles alongside the road.

As they pulled into Diana's driveway, and she saw her house, she started to cry. "*Oh, Fuck. Oh, Fuck.*" Michael parked the G63 as close as he could to the front door. They got out of the car.

Diana slowly said, "I had all my things in that house." Michael grabbed her hand and said, "They are just things, baby. We will get you new things." Diana got her key out and started for the front door. Michael grabbed her arm and said, "Hang on. See that?" He pointed to where the electric line from the street had been severed from the house and was lying across her front porch. Michael continued, "We can't go in there. If that cable goes live, the whole house could go up." Diana put her hands to her mouth. "*Oh, my God.*"

Michael led her by the hand back to the G63 and said, "Come on. Let's go to my mom's house. We have power and food. You can have a hot shower. We are probably going to have to live there for a while until we can sort out your house. We'll call the insurance company when we get there. We'll call the power company, too, and have them send out a repair crew, but they're probably going to be busy for a while." Michael gently pulled at Diana's hand and said, "Come on. Let's go."

Diana just stood there.

Michael said it again: "Come on, baby. Staring at it won't do you any good."

Diana started to cry. "I loved that house. It was the first house I ever owned."

Michael said again, "Let's go." Michael, still grasping Diana's hand, slowly led her back to the car.

By the time they pulled into the driveway, Sarah was home. They all hugged. Sarah said, "I just got home. It was busy last night, but it wasn't anything near what we were expecting. I'll go in later, when some of the casualties from the other islands start coming in."

Diana said that the same thing had happened to her. Michael told Sarah about Diana's house. Sarah hugged Diana and said, "Oh, that's terrible. You can stay here as long as you need. This is your home, too."

"Thank you, Sarah."

Sarah continued, "You must be exhausted. I'll put on a pot of coffee. Sarah went into the kitchen, came back out to Diana, gave her a key to the front door, and told her, "You are always welcome here."

Diana said, "Thank you."

Sarah said to Diana, "I'll get you some clothes that I think will fit."

Michael and Diana went into Michael's bedroom. They stripped off their clothes, wrapped towels around themselves, and walked down the hall to the bathroom, where they showered together. Both seemed to stay under the hot water for longer than usual. When they came out, Diana had changed into the clothes that Sarah had left her. Michael went out to the generator and briefly shut the unit down while he refilled the reservoir with gasoline. He looked into the house. No power. He restarted the generator, and the lights came back on.

Sarah was in the kitchen and asked Michael when he walked in, "How was it here last night?"

Michael told his mom, "The wind was howling, the rain was really intense, and the surf sounded really angry, but for the most part, it was uneventful. The neighbor has to remove his Hobie Cat from our backyard, and I want to show you something." Michael took his mom to the front of the house and showed her where the coconut had flown into the plywood that he'd placed over the window. He pointed to the plywood and said, "This was really the only damage."

Sarah was shocked. "Wow! I didn't see that when I came in. That board is absolutely crushed. That coconut could have caused a lot of damage to anyone who was inside."

Michael said, "Yep."

Sarah hugged Michael and said, "Thank you for caring for the old house. You're a lifesaver."

Michael said, "Mom, the old house saved my life. I'm convinced of this. Billy came over for a little bit last night. I bet he would say the same thing. It is a tough old house. It was built back in a time when they knew how to build houses."

Michael spent the next few hours removing all the plywood boards from the windows, and he had begun to rake the leaves up into piles in the front yard, but it would take a few more days of cleaning to get the yard back to any sense of order.

CHAPTER 37

Michael drove to the Yacht Club to check on the *Res Ipsa*. One of the docks had broken loose and had floated about 100 feet into Kaneohe Bay. Several big sailboats had come loose from their moorings and had grounded on the reef outside of the club. One had capsized on the reef, its keel sticking out of the water. The *Res Ipsa* was moored next to the other fishing boats, and they'd all been lashed together prior to the storm to prevent them from thrashing around in their moorings. For the most part, the hack worked. Some boats had minor damage. It looked like the *Res Ipsa* had survived another hurricane. One of the bilge pumps had become overwhelmed, and she was listing about 10 degrees to her starboard side. Michael climbed on board, entered the cabin, and engaged the pumps. It would take a few hours to right her.

The power came back on one day later. Slowly, the island was returning to normal. The small, loose debris was the first to be cleaned up. There was a massive undertaking by city sanitation engineers to remove the piles of debris that had been moved to the side of the road. Damage to homes and larger sitting debris would take a bit longer to be remediated. Diana moved in with Michael and Sarah. Insurance had arranged for tarps to be placed on the roof, and a chain-link construction fence was erected around the perimeter to help keep out anyone who did not have permission to be there. Prior to the fence going up, Diana was able to enter the house to retrieve some of her valuables. Most of the contents were severely waterlogged and would have to be destroyed. The house smelled like a damp rag. Water had gone into the walls and the wood frame of the house. In a few days, the house would start to turn moldy in the humidity. Diana packed up the things that were dry that had survived the storm. Michael bought a queen-sized bed and had it delivered to his mom's house.

Isaac heard about the storm and emailed his brother. *I am assuming that everything is okay? I didn't hear that the next Hawaii Court of Appeals judge was killed by a flying palm frond. Love, Isaac.*

Michael responded that everyone was fine but that Diana's house was not habitable at the moment. Michael went down to the beach, finding much debris on the sand and floating in the surf. Michael saw that a Taiwanese fishing boat had beached about a mile away from the house. Work crews were busy trying to get her back out to sea. Others were working on removing the debris.

The next morning, Michael got dressed with Diana and drove her back to Tripler. The sun was shining, and it was shaping up to be a beautiful Hawaii winter day. Diana was in a bit of a better mood, and they chatted for most of the drive. The roadblock out front was gone, and things were returning to normal at the big hospital. Michael drove Diana to the main entrance and said, "Have a good day at school, dear." They kissed. Michael said, "I'll see you at home later."

Diana said, "Okay. I'll check in with you throughout the day when I can."

Michael watched Diana walk up to the main entrance and quickly disappear. *Man, I love this woman*, Michael thought to himself.

He drove through downtown Honolulu and noticed that some of the office buildings had lost their windows and had been hastily boarded up to prevent any further damage. Michael drove through Waikiki, where there was little visible damage to the hotels, but some of the intersections were still clogged with sand. Some of the glass storefronts on Kalaukaua Avenue were boarded up. Past Diamond Head, he noticed that some of the houses had suffered fates similar to Diana's. *Had the hurricane intensified when it hit land, the damage would have been far worse*, Michael thought to himself.

Since Michael wasn't working, he was able to help Diana negotiate with her insurance company about her house. The insurance company started out determined to pay only claim-replacement value, but Michael had insisted that Diana's house had appreciated since the last appraisal, years ago, when Diana bought the house, and that the replacement value would not be sufficient. Michael told Diana that he would handle all interaction with the insurance company going forward. Diana hired him for the sum of $1, and she also told him that she would throw in some extra kisses. Diana was more than happy to cede this authority to Michael, and it gave Michael something to do so that he wouldn't be bored.

He met with the adjuster daily. Diana's house was determined to be a total loss. It helped that Michael was also a 25-year member of the same insurance company through his dad, as a military officer. They were actually a pleasure to deal with, compared with some other insurance companies he'd worked with over the years. The insurance company hired a remediation outfit to come in to clean what they could and remove all of Diana's things that were not salvageable. A new appraisal was ordered, based on neighborhood comps. Michael gave Diana daily and sometimes hourly updates.

After two weeks of negotiating with the insurance company, Michael called her at work when she had a light period at the clinic. "Hi."

"Hi!" Diana asked, "How is it going over there?"

Michael said, "Well, finally, some good news. The insurer and I have negotiated a pretty decent payout for you to rebuild your house. They are also giving you a bit more to replace your contents. You can buy some more Peacemaker Trading Company t-shirts."

Diana said, "You're cute."

Michael continued, "Maybe we should hire an architect and completely redesign the house, make it into something beautiful. Remember Roger Sullivan from BU? He moved back here to take over his dad's architect firm. We can call him." Roger Sullivan had gone to school with Michael and became his roommate when they all rented a walkup apartment in an old brownstone in Brighton, close to BU on the Green Line. In the winter, the old radiators would rattle like a bag of bones, which always would amuse Michael, as he'd grown up in Hawaii and had never even seen a radiator until he went to Boston for college.

Diana said, "We can talk to him. What did you have in mind?"

Michael said, "All I know is that I would want to keep the hot tub. That hot tub has exponentially increased my sex life a thousand-fold."

Diana giggled. "Now you're talking! I've used that hot tub more with you than I ever have. Doug actually hated it—said it made him feel like an old person."

Michael snorted and said, "Um, yeah. What did you see in him, again? Hot tubs are essential."

Diana giggled.

Michael continued, "They are going to direct-deposit the check into your bank account the day after tomorrow. Don't be surprised. It's kind of a large amount."

Diana was curious. "*How large?*"

Michael said, "Let's just say that it is close to seven figures."

Diana screamed, "*Holy fuck!*"

Michael laughed, and Diana continued, "We weren't even close to that a few days ago. I am going to like having a lawyer in the family. I will definitely pay you back tonight—wink, wink."

Michael told Diana, "We had many discussions about the actual replacement cost that was based on how much your house has appreciated in the past few years. *Lucky you live in Hawaii*, as they say. The crazy housing prices here definitely helped. We can start demolition soon. We're probably going to have to get a bridge loan or some mezzanine financing to help, but we should get you pretty close to your dream house. I have some money saved. I can help a little."

Diana said, "I was already in my dream house."

Michael said, "Tonight, let's sit down and decide what we want in a house, really give it some thought."

Diana thought about it and said, "I love that idea."

CHAPTER 38

Michael, Diana, and Sarah celebrated the first night of Hanukkah. They sat around and drank and made *latkes*, ate stuffed cabbage that Sarah made, listened to music, laughed at life, and for a brief moment, forget about the events of the past few months. Michael got his mom a sterling silver John Hardy cuff and some Chanel perfume, because he knew that his mom loved both. Sarah got him an iTunes gift card and some new surf trunks. Diana got Michael a new re-issue of the complete Bob Marley boxed set with new song additions, and two whimsical Ferragamo ties. Michael handed Diana a skinny black box with a big red bow. "Happy Hanukkah, baby."

"Michael, I was just kidding. I didn't want anything."

Michael said, "I know, and you're not always going to get awesome presents like this, but I had to do it."

Diana opened the box and gasped when she saw the strand of Tahitian pearls. "Michael, they are beautiful," Diana said quietly.

Michael responded, "I have friends in low places. My buddy handpicked this strand for you."

Diana looked at Sarah and said, "Were you in on this?"

Sarah, as surprised as Diana, responded, "No—when my son gets a bug up his ass to do something, he does it by himself."

"Michael, they are incredible pearls." Diana got up and kissed Michael.

Michael said, "You got some seriously good loot this year."

Diana said, "Yes, but the best was you."

Michael was running an errand in Kailua town when his phone rang. It was Marvin Chong. *Okay, here we go.*

"*Boychik.*"

"Marvin."

Marvin continued, "What did your Uncle Marvin tell you about the Court of Appeals position?"

Michael said, "Not to worry about it?"

Marvin said in response, "*Not to worry about it.*"

Michael's heart started pounding.

Marvin said, "At 6 PM tonight, turn on the local news."

Michael was overwhelmed. "Marvin, I don't know what to say. I'm honored."

Marvin said, "Say 'Thank you. I accept.'"

Michael said, humbly, "Thank you. I accept."

Marvin, in a proud moment, said, "You will be a great judge, *boychik.*"

Michael called Sarah. "Mom, turn on the news tonight at 6 PM."

Sarah said, "Why?"

Michael said, "You'll see."

Michael called Billy. "Yo."

"*Yo.*"

Michael said, "Turn on the news tonight at 6 PM."

Billy said, excitedly, "*Seriously?*"

Michael told his friend, "Yep."

Billy said, "Holy shit! That's awesome! I mean, holy shit! That's awesome, *Your Honor.* Congratulations!"

"Thank you."

Billy said, "You'll make a great judge. It's in your blood."

Michael said, "Thank you, buddy." Michael texted his sister to check one of the Hawaii news channels later online, that she would see a familiar name.

Diana came home early. Michael was sitting on the couch reading a magazine. He told her, "Hey, let's go to Buzz's."

Diana, putting down her bags, said, "Okay, sure."

Michael said, "Let's go *right now.*"

Diana looked at him, a little annoyed. "Can I change first?"

Michael said, "Yes, but make it quick."

Diana saw him look at his watch. Diana, walking from the hallway to Michael's bedroom said, "Okay, *Rain Man*—I'll make it quick."

Michael followed her to the doorway of his bedroom and said, "Come on!"

Diana said, exasperatedly, "Michael, do you want me to go like this?" She came out naked except for a pair of panties. Michael said, "Well, sure. I bet we'll get a free meal."

Diana said, "Or *arrested.*"

Michael said, "*You'll* get arrested. *I'll* get a free meal."

Diana got dressed. She didn't have many clothes at the Grand house, as most of her clothes had been ruined. She threw on a floral print dress.

Michael said to Diana, "Want to drive?"

Michael handed her the key fob to the G63. Initially, Diana wrinkled her nose, but when she climbed in and sat in front of the steering wheel of the G63, she let out a little giggle. She started the engine, she heard the exhaust growl, and she giggled again. She put the G63 in reverse and stepped on the gas, the car roared and flew backwards before Diana stepped on the brake.

Michael said, "Easy, tiger. This car has almost 600 foot-pounds of torque."

Diana turned the car around and stepped on the gas, and they flew out of the Grands' driveway on to Kalaheo Road. Pulling in to Buzz's, Diana purposefully drove up a curb. The big truck took it in stride and easily climbed over it. Diana said, "Whoa, I didn't even feel that!"

Michael grinned and said, "I told you. You're going to want to drive the big boy now all the time."

Diana looked like a kid unwrapping a big birthday present.

Michael said, "Come on. Let's park. Come on!"

Diana looked at him like a parent mad at a hyperactive child and said, "Michael David Grand, what the fuck has gotten into you? You have *shpilkes* tonight."

Michael grinned again and said, "You'll see."

Michael had a seat reserved by the bar. They sat down so that Diana was facing the flat-screen TV that was above the bartender. Diana was talking to Michael, and she suddenly became distracted. Michael said to her, "*Hello?* I'm over here." Michael had a smile on his face.

Diana was fully focused on the TV news story. She got up, walked over to the bar, and asked the bartender if he could turn up the sound.

Michael turned around; he saw his photo on TV and heard something about how he'd been nominated by the Governor to fill his late father's seat on the Hawaii State Court of Appeals. Michael started to tear up.

The story ended. Diana came back to the table and looked at Michael, beaming.

Michael said to her, "I wanted it to be a surprise. I don't have it yet. I still have to be confirmed."

Diana said, "It was a surprise. You'll be confirmed. Everyone loved your dad, and people here love you, too. I love you. You'll be a great judge. Your dad would have been very proud of you." Diana leaned across the table to kiss him. She said, "We have celebrated some seriously awesome events at this restaurant."

Michael said, "Hopefully, there will be many more to come." The bartender came over, brought them a bottle of champagne on the house, and shook Michael's hand, congratulating him.

Confirmation hearings were set for two weeks in the future. During the hearings with the Senate Judiciary committee, Michael stated that he was deeply honored to be nominated to the seat held by his father, that he treasured the opportunity to honor his memory and legacy as an appellate court judge. Michael stressed his respect for the letter of the law and for precedent. When asked about his lack of any prior judicial experience, Michael pivoted to argue that he had worked with some of the best judges and lawyers in the country and that he would be a "lawyer's judge," as he had long-standing relationships with many of the attorneys in the state. In the end, the Judiciary Committee unanimously recommended Michael to be confirmed, and his confirmation was sent to the entire Senate for voting.

CHAPTER 39

Exactly three months to the day after his father died, Michael Grand was confirmed as the next Appellate Judge for the State of Hawaii. When Michael was sworn in by the Chief Justice, Michael's family, friends, co-workers, other attorneys, and strangers all joined him for this milestone event. Tradition when events are celebrated in Hawaii is the giving of a lei. There were so many lei—*Maile lei, tuberose lei, pikake lei, double- and triple-strand orchid lei*—that they were stacked up almost to his nose. Michael could barely breathe without smelling Hawaii. Isaac sent Michael an email. *I wish I could have been there, brother. Does this mean that I won't ever get a speeding ticket again? Love, Isaac.*

Michael and Diana went to Buzz's that night. Over Hinanos and grilled Mahi, Diana presented Michael with a gift. Michael opened the wrapped box and saw that Diana had gotten him a British judge's wig and a beautiful gavel made of rare *curly koa*. Diana asked, "Why don't judges wear those things anymore? I think they are kind of cool."

Michael responded, "American judges used to wear wigs, but they stopped doing so in the 19th century, mostly to show that America was a democratic institution that no longer followed the rigid rules imposed under the British judicial system." He put the wig on.

Diana started giggling and said, "That's a good look for you!"

Michael felt like a clown and said, "I feel like something out of a Gilbert and Sullivan opera."

Diana stood up in the restaurant and sang out, "All hail great judge!" and sat back down.

Michael giggled. He was a Gilbert and Sullivan super fan and immediately caught the reference to *Trial by Jury*. Michael said, "Clever girl."

Diana stood up again and curtsied. After dinner, Diana asked if she could drive home.

Michael handed her the keys to the G63 and said, "I told you."

Diana climbed up to the driver's seat and said, "Man, I love driving this thing. I love sitting up so high, I can see everything."

Michael said, "Maybe it's time to trade in the LS."

Diana responded, "Maybe."

Michael said, "Next time you're on base, stop and get a sticker for the windshield with one of those little birdie symbols. You can drive it when I'm wanting to drive the 280SL."

The next day, Michael and Diana met with Roger Sullivan. He was happy to see them both and was thrilled that they were getting married. Roger said, "I always knew you two would wind up together." For Diana's house, Roger proposed a vintage look but with a modern feel, something with plenty of light and tall ceilings, but with an upstairs master bedroom and wraparound upper and lower lanais. He wanted to increase the square footage and would work with a land-scape architect to make Diana's house something beautiful. Diana's only request was that Roger build the house strong enough that the roof wouldn't blow off in the next storm.

Michael said that he wanted a gourmet kitchen, a three-car garage, and most importantly, a wood-fired hot tub. He turned to Diana, and she winked at him. Roger said that he would get back to them in about a month with preliminary drawings.

Michael wasn't required to start his new job for another month. He used this time to recharge his batteries. He walked the beach. Diana hooked him up with a private tour of the USS *Missouri*, and he was blown away by the massive battleship. Diana also had a colleague who was married to the head of the National Park Service in Pearl Harbor. He gave Michael a special tour of the area on Ford Island that is normally off limits, where they placed the superstructure of the USS *Arizona* after the *Arizona* was salvaged following the attack on December 7th, 1941.

Once, Isaac told Michael that it was his greatest honor to be able to dive on the wreck of the USS *Arizona* with some Navy diver friends, and afterwards, he became very emotional. Michael knew why—he always choked up upon going to the USS *Arizona* memorial. On that day, staring at and touching the rusted remains of the USS *Arizona's* superstructure, he started to tear up.

Michael and Diana stayed in Waikiki for the weekend and pretended they were tourists. They walked Waikiki beach, bought souvenirs, visited Shangri-La, the beautiful Islamic-style mansion owned by Doris Duke at the foot of Diamond Head, and stayed in bed in their hotel room, ordering room service. Michael drove out the North Shore, took the G63 up a muddy old fire road through a forest near a Boy Scout camp, and put the car through its paces.

Afterwards, he ate at *Cholo's* in Haleiwa because he wanted the best *Ahi* burrito on the planet. He stopped at Matsumoto's for some *shave ice* with vanilla ice cream and *azuki* bean, and went to Patagonia to buy some t-shirts before he turned right and headed home.

Michael stopped at the prawn farm on the way and bought three pounds of fresh prawns for dinner. Michael hiked up the steps to the top of Diamond Head. Michael visited his old high school and was amazed to see that some of his teachers were still there. Michael and Billy went day fishing off the *Res Ipsa* while the entire state was working around them. Michael, Diana, and Sarah would usually eat dinner together outside on the lanai.

One night after they got home from a movie, Michael and Diana were lying in Michael's bed. Michael was half under the covers and had his head next to Diana's ear, his chin on her neck. He was rubbing her ear. Michael said, "We're not getting any younger. Have you ever thought about kids?"

Diana, with eyes closed, said, "Michael, you know I'm still infertile—right? It doesn't get better through magic." As a child, Diana had her fallopian tubes severely scarred after she had a ruptured appendix. Michael knew this on their fifth date. "Of course, I do, but we could adopt, we could get another Isaac or two. As far as I can tell, I think I was put on this earth for two reasons. The first was to marry you, and the second was to be a dad like my dad was to me."

Diana started sobbing and put a pillow over her head so that Sarah would not hear her crying. Michael continued to rub Diana's ear and then lifted up the pillow. Tears were running down Diana's face.

Diana looked at him and said, "I was always worried about this conversation, especially after I fell in love with your parents and saw what amazing people they were. I figured that they wanted grand-children and that I could not make them happy."

Michael, responded, lovingly, and said, "Diana, I told my parents that you couldn't have kids when I brought you to Hawaii the first time. They've known about this for years. It meant nothing to them. They are huge fans of adoption, obviously. They loved you because you were you."

Diana started crying again.

Michael comforted his fiancée. "Baby, at the end of the day, I still want to spend the rest of my life with you. I thought that we could figure it out later."

Diana was crying harder.

Michael said, "Honey, this is a good thing. We're good. If it doesn't happen, it doesn't happen, but it sure would be nice to bring some love to a kid who didn't ever think they would get it."

Diana was staring at the ceiling, tears running down the side of her face, her blond hair in a mop on the pillow. Michael continued, "We could talk about it some more."

Diana turned to put her face against Michael's neck. "I'm flawed, and you and your family still love me."

"Diana, you're not 'flawed.' You're perfect the way you are. I also think you would be a good mom. I see it in your eyes. I have seen how loving you can be. I am also kind of a big kid. It would be fun to be a big kid with kids. It would be nice to take this journey with you and a family."

Diana got out of bed to blow her nose, her face completely red. She bent down to pick up Michael's t-shirt that was crumpled at the foot of the bed and put it on as she walked to the door.

Michael watched as she opened the bedroom door and walked to the bathroom down the hall.

Diana came back in a few minutes later, climbed back into bed, and spooned with Michael. Diana wasn't mad that Michael had, years ago, shared her most intimate secret with his family. On the contrary, she was relieved. She was almost embarrassed that she had used this as an excuse to move on from Michael, and she never told him this. "I am so fortunate to have found a family. I have been alone for a long time."

Michael reached over and started making a slow circle on Diana's stomach with his fingers. "Diana, we all love you. We want you to be happy and at peace with yourself."

Diana turned to Michael and said to him, "And you still wanted to marry me?"

Without hesitation, Michael said, "Diana, I told you years ago that this wasn't a big deal. It still isn't a big deal."

Diana kissed Michael and said, "I love *this* man."

Michael kissed Diana and said, "I'm the same guy I have always been. I have been in love with you from the first day I ever saw you. That was a long time ago. That hasn't changed."

Diana looked at Michael and responded, "You are the best thing that has ever happened to me."

Michael watched Diana fall asleep with a smile on her face. It was the last thing Michael remembered before he, too, fell asleep.

CHAPTER 40

om Young called Michael. Michael answered on the
second ring. Tom was from one of the oldest, most-
established families in Hawaii, descended from the original mission-
aries who came to settle the islands in the early 1800s. The Youngs
had befriended generations of Hawaiian Kings and Queens and for
their loyalty were either given or were able to purchase large tracts
of land. Tom and Michael had gone to high school and law school
together. Tom's family owned a house in Vail, and Michael had spent
many weekends there skiing with Tom and his family.

Michael and Tom were still friends despite long gaps in their
friendship. After law school, Tom moved back to Hawaii to become
the general counsel for the entity that managed his family's large land
holdings both in Hawaii and on the mainland. When Tom's dad
died, he became the CEO and Chairman of the Board. Tom invited
Michael to come mountain biking at the family-owned ranch the next
day. Michael said he would be thrilled to accept. Aside from the legal
connection, the two of them shared a true love of wine. Shortly after
Michael moved to Atlanta, he defended the daughter of a rich client

on a DUI charge. Michael got the woman off and then worked with her dad to get her into one of the best rehabs in the country. As a token of his appreciation, her father, whose family owned one of the largest wine and liquor distributors in the country, sent Michael and a guest on a two-week wine tasting through Bordeaux. Michael took Tom, and the two of them spent their time meeting with Chateau owners, sommeliers, chief winemakers, and industry reps, tasting their way across the region. It was a once-in-a-lifetime opportunity that neither of them ever forgot.

That evening, Michael went out to the garage and looked at his mountain bikes. The Young family's ranch was one of Michael's favorite places in the world to ride. Growing up in Hawaii made Michael a strong, technical mountain biker, since most of the rides there were rocky, narrow, wet mountain trails. The Young ranch, with its more than 4000 acres, contained technical trails, river crossings, steep climbs, crazy descents, old jeep trails, the remnants of an old airfield and multi-level bunkers with still fully active large elevators, left over from World War Two. Tom once said that the guns from the USS *Arizona* were briefly stored in one of the larger bunkers after they were removed from the warship in the early months of 1942.

Michael knew the terrain, and despite the technical riding, opted for his titanium hardtail over his fully suspended rig. Michael inflated the tires and loaded the mountain bike and his gear into the back of the G63.

The next morning, Michael rode out to the Youngs' ranch. He drove past the main buildings, where tourists could rent ATVs or go on jeep tours that would emulate the memorable scenes from several blockbuster films that were shot on location at the ranch. He drove about two miles down the single-lane road next to the beach and turned left at a rusted, old locked gate that was blocking a well-worn dirt access road. Tom parked his twenty-year-old Land Cruiser in front of the open gate. The old truck didn't give anyone the slightest notion that Tom was personally worth eight figures. That was a common theme in Hawaii: if you saw some guy driving down the road in a twenty-year-old car and you didn't know that he came from one of Hawaii's richest families, you would think that he was just another *Haole* going to the beach. In the current days of constant "look-at-me," Tom had not even one social media account. Michael pulled his G63 next to the Land Cruiser, parked, and turned off the engine.

Tom opened the rear gate of his Land Cruiser, and his three-year old Chesapeake Bay Retriever jumped out, tail wagging, and trotted over to Michael. Michael bent over to pet the dog behind its ears. "That's Jeffrey," said Tom.

"Hi, Jeffrey," said Michael.

"Jeffrey is going to be our guide today. He loves it up here." Tom walked over to Michael, and they hugged.

"It's good to see you."

"It's good to see you, too. I went to your dad's funeral, but I didn't come over to you because, when my dad died, I didn't really want anyone coming over to me, and I wanted to give you your space."

"I appreciate that," said Michael.

Tom and Michael got their bikes ready and locked their cars. They rode behind the gate, and Tom got off his bike and walked back to lock it, Jeffrey following right behind. Today, Michael would have a private tour. They started out riding the dirt access road, up a small incline. Jeffrey ran up ahead. After about a half-mile, the jeep trail entered into a large grassy area, several hundred acres, that was surrounded by ancient volcanic mountains that were jutting out all around them. They were in a lush, green valley. It started to drizzle when they passed by a herd of cattle walking in a large meadow. In addition to being a tourist destination, the Young Ranch was also a working ranch. They rode through an area that was completely deforested from the storm. The remnants of several large trees were neatly stacked in large, chopped woodpiles.

Tom came up to a river crossing and stopped. The water was flowing, but not rapidly. Jeffrey was there, waiting for them and had started to drink some of the water in the river that flowed down from the mountain. Tom was able to gauge that the current was not that strong and crossed the river. Jeffrey jumped in and was immediately in water up to his lower chest and slowly dog-paddled across, his tail floating on the water straight out behind him, like a rudder on a boat. When Jeffrey had crossed, he immediately shook himself off and ran up ahead. Michael shifted into a lower gear and slowly pedaled across.

Michael and Tom were riding side by side the access road for the next mile. The climb became steeper, and the two of them were talking and catching up as they pedaled.

"How's your sister?"

Tom's sister was Michael's first love. He'd taken her to the prom.

"Meredith is a Senior Vice President at Google and is married to a neurosurgeon. They have three kids. She sits on our corporate board of directors."

Michael said, "You can always tell the winners at the starting gate." Meredith had gone to Harvard both for undergraduate and business school. "Please give her my regards."

Tom said, "Of course."

Jeffrey had found a stick lying in the road. It was almost as big as him, but it didn't matter. He picked it up in his mouth and proudly trotted off with it. The rain had started coming down harder, and soon both Tom and Michael were covered in mud. They came up to what looked like an old Victorian two-story house painted green but, in reality, was a movie set for a television show that was filmed at the ranch in the early 1990s. Inside, the building was completely void of rooms. Tom rode over, got off his bike, walked up the stairs to a covered front lanai, and sat down to watch the rain. Michael followed, and, a few minutes later, Jeffrey appeared—minus his stick—ran up the stairs, and shook off his water and mud onto Tom and Michael.

Tom reached into his backpack, removed a bottle of wine, grabbed two glasses and a corkscrew, and proceeded to open the bottle. Tom had one of the best wine cellars in the world, and he had developed a sophisticated palate over the years. Tom knew that Michael's wine knowledge was pretty good. He opened the bottle, smelled the cork, and then poured some in one of the glasses, swirled it around, and smelled the wine. "Yum." He poured a glass for Michael.

Michael took it and turned the bottle so that he could see the label. "Um, buddy, that is a 1982 Latour." Michael knew that it was a perfect vintage and that it cost more than $2000 a bottle.

"Oh, I thought I grabbed the 2000."

Michael smelled into the glass and said, "In the middle of a ranch, covered in mud, and soaking wet, we are drinking a 1982 Latour. What the fuck!"

Tom responded, "Now is as good a time as any. I thought that you would appreciate this bottle. I gladly share my wine with people who understand it."

Michael said, "Are you going to tell me that it has notes of pork fat, charcoal, lush blueberries, and turmeric?" Michael said, half-jokingly.

"Nope. I'm going to tell you that it is really fucking good."

Michael sat with his friend, drinking one of the best bottles of wine of all time.

Tom was silent, savoring his wine.

Michael watched the rain pouring down, listening to the sound it made as it hit the house. "On my nice-moments list, this one is right up there," said Michael. He told Tom about Diana.

Tom was truly glad for his friend. Michael sat there, staring out at the beauty around him and said, "Buddy, I hope you never get rid of this place. It would be sad to see that one day it's become condos."

Tom, looking into his wine glass said, "As long as I'm alive, as long as my children are alive, that will never happen. Meredith fully supports this decision."

Michael continued drinking his glass of wine.

Tom continued, "Do you see that opening up about 800 feet near the top of that crest?" Tom pointed at about one o'clock.

Michael responded, "Yep. It looks like a cave."

Tom told his friend, "It's a burial cave. Years ago, we had a groundskeeper who worked for us; he was pure Hawaiian. His father was a groundskeeper here, as was his father before him. One day, he was hiking up there and went into the cave and found the bones. Hawaiians believe that the bones of their ancestors, and the land they are buried in, is sacred. When he discovered what he found, he exited the cave, shaking and visibly upset. The next day, he woke up to discover that his hair had gone completely white. He was 35. We had a *Kahuna* come up and bless the area, and we left the bones where they were. Michael, this land is sacred, and we want to keep it the way it is. We want it to stay in the family."

Michael, visibly moved by the story said, "Buddy, I am so glad that you are not like all the other landowners who only want to monetize what they have."

Tom continued, "The family has more than we will ever need, even the cousins and distant-cousins will be cared for. This land is going to stay the way it is."

Tom poured the last of the bottle into Michael's glass. "You're going to make a great judge, Michael. I'm proud to call you my friend."

"Thank you, Tom. I was humbled to be picked. It's a great tribute to my dad."

Tom continued, "So, I'm assuming that you're staying in Hawaii for a while? You're not going to run back to Atlanta, again?"

Michael responded, "Tom, this is my home. This is a part of my DNA. I was born here. I'm going to die here. It took my leaving here to figure that out."

Tom said, "Well, my friend, it sounds like that woman of yours finally talked some sense into you." They clinked glasses.

The rain had slowed to a drizzle, and the two finished up the wine and stood up. Jeffrey ran down the stairs and went right for a giant puddle and rolled around, exiting completely covered in mud. Tom said to the dog, "I'm throwing you in the ocean when we get home—you're not coming into the house like that!" The two rode back to their cars. Tom invited Michael and Diana to his second son's first-year baby luau at the end of the month. Michael said that he would love to attend. Tom and Michael hugged.

Tom said to Michael, "I'm glad that we were able to rekindle our friendship where we left off."

Michael said, "Me, too. Thanks for thinking of me today. I'm going to remember this day for a very long time." Michael drove home replaying the details of the day in his head, and he thought how very lucky he was.

CHAPTER 41

Grief sometimes takes a long, lazy, and uneven trajectory. Michael Grand missed his dad. He missed his calm voice, his always-wise advice. He decided that it was time to go visit his dad. One day on a pretty, cloudy Memorial Day, Michael drove to the Chinese cemetery in Manoa to visit the family plot. He stopped at Andy's and grabbed a turkey, avocado, tomato, and cheese sandwich, parked, and walked to the Grand family gravesite. Years ago, Joshua had had a bench erected in front of the tombstone, so that he could sit and visit with his parents. Michael reached into the pocket of his slacks and pulled out a smooth stone that he had found while walking the beach one day and thought that his dad would like it.

He placed it on top of the tombstone with the other stones that had been placed there by Sarah, who went to the gravesite frequently. He also placed two other rocks on the tombs of his grandfather and grandmother. It was a Jewish custom to place stones on the graves of loved ones to symbolize the persistence of memory—that the deceased will never be forgotten. Some Jews believed that the placement of rocks would keep the soul of the deceased in this world. Michael reached into his briefcase, pulled out a small American flag on a stick, planted it in the ground in front of his dad's tombstone, and said, "Thank you for your service, dad. If you were not in the Navy, I would never have been born."

Michael sat down on the bench and ate his sandwich and thought that his grandfather was right—that it was so pretty in this spot. Michael started talking to his dad. "Hi, dad. Sorry I couldn't come sooner. I was a little busy. But you knew that. Somehow, I think you had something to do with me getting engaged to Diana and getting confirmed to fill your seat on the bench. I miss you. I think about you all the time."

Michael started to tear up. "I love you. The world is so different without you in it. I want to honor you every day when I do the job that you did so well, that defined you, for so many years." Michael opened the flap of his briefcase and pulled out a rough draft of one of the first decisions he would author as a Hawaii State appellate court judge and started reading the words. Even now, Michael and Joshua would review cases together. Just then, it started to rain, because it always rains in Manoa. The rain washed away Michael's tears, and Michael sat on the bench until he was soaked and started shivering from cold. Michael told his dad that he would come back to visit on a regular basis.

The plans on Diana's house were amended and finally approved and construction started. Diana discovered that she liked to drive to the house at the end of the day to see what progress had been made. For the first time in her life, Diana felt that her life was settled. She felt happy.

Michael's new job allowed him to come home at a sensible hour almost every day. Michael, too, would stop by the house every day after work. Sometimes he would catch the crew still working. Sometimes he would see his fiancée there. Not today. Michael went home to his mom's house and saw Diana's car parked on the grass in front. Sarah wasn't home yet. Diana was in Michael's bedroom, changing into her bikini and surf trunks. She said, "Let's go walk the beach."

Michael said, "Give me five minutes to change." They walked the beach holding hands.

Michael could sense some hesitation with Diana. He said, "What's up, sailor?"

Diana responded, "Not sure."

Michael stopped walking and said to Diana, "Are you sick?"

Diana shook her head and said, "Oh, no. Nothing like that."

Michael said, "Did you go back with the proctologist?"

Diana looked at him and rolled her eyes, "*Oh, please.* Give me a little credit, would you?"

Michael asked again, "What's up, Doc?"

Diana sat down on the beach. Michael sat next to her. They stared out at the calm ocean. Diana said, "I got orders today. Landstuhl. For six months. They need some intensivists to help manage the influx of critical patients coming in from Afghanistan. They had a slow period for a while, but they are seeing an increase in casualties."

Michael said, "So what's the problem?"

Diana said, "First of all, the Navy promised me last time I deployed that it would be the last time."

Michael said, "You believed them?"

Diana sighed, "I guess I did." She continued, "Second, I don't want to leave *us.* We'll have to delay the wedding until I get back."

Michael responded, "Big fucking deal. We're talking about a few months' delay from June."

Diana was still processing Michael's response, "Who's going to manage the house construction?"

Michael said, "I'll be here. I'll talk to the contractor every day."

Diana said, "I'm not so sure I want to go."

"Diana, they'll court-martial you if you don't go. I am a halfway decent lawyer, but I don't want to defend you on that."

Diana continued, "Years ago, when I was single, I loved being deployed. Now, I'm not so sure."

Michael looked at Diana and said, "We've done the long-distance thing before."

Diana said, "For six fucking weeks. How are we going to do this for six months? The last time didn't work out so well—remember?"

Michael tried to reassure his fiancée. "Hey, at the end of the day, if you still want to come back to me, we can do anything."

Diana said, "Deployments are hard."

Michael said, "Diana, we can make this work. My mom and dad were married when he was in Vietnam. They made it work."

Diana said, "Michael, the Navy has been very good to me, and I love it almost as much as I love you, but sometimes the Navy takes the fun out of life."

Michael stood up, shook the sand off his surf trunks, and said, "Well, the way I see it, you have two choices. First, you can deploy, and we figure it out, or you can resign your commission. Have you made your 20 yet?"

Diana said, "I have a year to go."

Michael continued, "Okay, so you have one option. You deploy."

Diana said, "What about us? I'm worried that we'll fall apart and go back to not talking to each other."

Michael looked at Diana and said, "Baby, we can make anything work for six months. Do you still want to marry me?"

Diana said, "Of course, I do."

Michael told her, "Well, then it's settled. You have to go. At least it's not to Afghanistan."

Diana responded, "Michael, my time in Afghanistan was the most important of my career. I was honored to be a part of the effort there."

Michael looked at Diana and said, "Sorry. I didn't mean it like that. I meant that I won't have to worry about the Taliban trying to shoot your ass."

They held hands and starting walking again.

Michael asked Diana, "When do you have to leave?"

Diana said, "Two weeks."

Michael thought about it and said, "I just started my new job, and I don't think I can get much vacation time, but I have always wanted to drive really fast on the Autobahn. This is a bucket-list item. Even if it's just for a few days, I can come visit."

Diana said, "I would love for you to visit me in Germany."

Michael stopped again and looked at Diana. She looked back at him.

Michael said, "Of course, there is *another option*."

Diana said, "What is that?"

Michael said, "We can get married *before* you leave. That would give you a good reason to come back."

Diana said, "What about Isaac being your best man?"

Michael said, "He'll get over it, and maybe we can have a big party when you get back. I'll email him tonight. What do you think?"

Diana was beaming and said, "I think that you are the most amazing man I have ever met. You would still want to keep me around even if I deployed?"

Michael said, "I keep trying to tell you that this is no big fucking deal. You're worth it."

Diana said, "I wish I'd known that six years ago. My life would have been very different."

Michael said, "You're telling *me*, sailor."

They got to the house, and Michael said, "I think you should go. I hear Germany is awesome."

Diana said, "I don't know how much of Germany I'll get to see."

Michael crossed his arms and said, "That's it. I'm ruling on my first opinion as a sitting judge. You're going. Will you give some thought to getting married early?"

Diana said, "Yes. I'll be lonely, but I'll get over it."

Michael kissed Diana and said, "There is a new invention called the mobile phone. We could FaceTime. I might have to jerk off more, but we'll be okay."

Diana giggled.

Michael continued, "Diana, you have to go. On the day that you hit your 20, if you want to retire then, so be it. But you have to go. It is not worth losing everything that you have worked so hard for. Let's go get some dinner. I'm ravenous."

Diana said, "I'll buy."

Michael said, "Deal."

That night, Michael emailed Isaac and told him what was going on. The next day, Isaac responded. *Not surprised the Navy jerked her around. They are good at that. I don't need to be your best man to have your back. If you want to get married early, I won't be offended. Love, Isaac.*

CHAPTER 42

The next morning, Diana told Michael that she wanted to get married before she deployed.

Michael said, "My mom will stroke if we go off to city hall and elope. She will want some kind of official ceremony and a party. Let's see if we can get anything together in two weeks. Man, most people plan their wedding for months or years."

Diana said, "As long as I have you, that's all that I want. I don't need anything big."

Michael called his mom. Within 20 minutes, Sarah spun into action and began planning the party. They would make this work. Michael called Harry and ordered a white gold band with diamonds for the wedding ring.

Four days before Diana deployed, the Chief Justice of the Hawaii Supreme Court married Diana and Michael on the beach behind the Grand house at sunset. Diana wore a simple dress and a *Haku Lei* on her head. Michael wore one of his dad's favorite aloha shirts and a pair of khaki pants and a *Maile Lei*. Both were barefoot. Sarah,

Billy and Kimberly, Marvin Chong and his wife, Alison, Harry and Alexandra, Tom and his wife, Laura, were all there.

Afterwards, everyone went to a private room in a Chinese restaurant in Chinatown and had a 10-course meal. Later, Diana and Michael were in bed.

Michael said, "How do you feel?"

Diana said, "Happy. How do you feel?

Michael said, "*Complete*."

Michael and Diana Grand spent the first night of their marriage in the same room that Michael had grown up in.

On the day that Diana deployed, she and Michael got up early, watched the sunrise off of Kailua beach, and lounged around the house all morning. Then they got dressed, and Michael took her down to River Street for the best *Pho* on the planet. Diana was visibly melancholic.

Michael said, "It's only for six months."

Diana said, "I know, but I don't want to leave you."

Michael responded, "I don't want to leave you, either, but we have the rest of our lives to be together."

Diana started to cry. Michael said, "It'll be fine. Besides, I'll spend some good, quality time with my mom and my brother. He should be back before you come home."

Diana looked at Michael and said, "I love you."

Michael said, "Right back at you, kid."

Michael drove Diana to the C-17 that was on the tarmac at Hickam. They kissed and hugged.

Diana was crying. "I love you."

"I love you. You better FaceTime me."

"I will."

Diana grabbed her bags and turned and walked to the plane; she looked back at Michael. Michael waved to her. Michael stood there until the C-17 took off. He got into the G63, and he drove home, sad.

Life went on for Michael Grand. Michael would send Diana daily pictures of the house, which was slated to be finished around the time that she would return from Landstuhl. Michael was invited to join the monthly poker game that his dad used to play. The Chief of Police, the Chief Justice, the President of the Medical Staff at Queen's Medical Center, Marvin, and a famous local celebrity all sat around the poker table on the first Friday of the month. Michael missed his wife. Diana missed her husband.

Michael was able to visit Diana in Germany for a very long weekend. Michael flew from Honolulu to San Francisco to Frankfurt, almost without stopping. He felt like Isaac, flying halfway around the world to be there for his family. This is what family did, and Michael was so very fortunate to have all of these wonderful people in his life—although, he was tired as hell after the long flight.

In Germany, Diana purchased her own G63. Michael wanted Diana to get the less-powerful G550, but she loved how the G63 sounded. Michael rented a car. He was so surprised that they gave him an E Class Mercedes as a rental car, as this car would never happen in the States, and drove the two hours to Affalterbach, the spiritual home of AMG, the legendary tuning arm of Mercedes Benz. He and Diana went through a factory tour and sat down with the factory reps to design Diana's G63. Diana opted for the pearl-white model with a cognac interior. Diana arranged the car to be shipped back to her house in Kailua, which would be there when she arrived home.

Michael went into the factory shop and loaded himself with AMG gear. He told one of the nice factory reps that he'd always wanted to take a big car out on the Autobahn. Mercedes very graciously honored his request. They let Michael test-drive a brand-new $250,000 S65, with a factory driver sitting in the passenger seat. Michael was amazed at how such a large automobile could go so fast. The S65's big bi-turbo V-12 sounded like an angry gorilla pounding on the engine block. The Mercedes factory driver was shouting encouragement to Michael. "Go faster, Michael! Push it, Michael!" Michael looked down at the speedometer; it read 300 kph. Michael had a smile on his face.

Michael spent the next day touring the giant hospital complex and met some of the people Diana worked with. He was sad to leave his wife and thought about her and their recent experience together for the entire flight back to the States, when he wasn't sleeping.

Michael sold Diana's old LS 400 to a high school kid for $1500. Michael put a "Navy Wife" license-plate holder that he found at the Pearl Harbor commissary on his G63, mostly as a joke, but the shoe fit. Michael *was* a Navy wife. Michael and Diana spoke, emailed, or FaceTimed almost every day. They would talk about the house and last-minute ideas or additions. Diana became less sad and really liked working with a great bunch of people in the big hospital in Germany. Michael loved his new job, and, once, he felt a presence and thought that his dad was standing behind him with his hand on Michael's shoulder. Michael couldn't explain the feeling, and that night he told Sarah about it. She just assumed that it was his dad, saying "Hello."

Michael contacted his sister at least once a week. In some ways, they had become closer since Joshua's death. Michael was always there to give Janice advice. Divorce was hard on her, but she bought a place close to work with plenty of room for the kids. She threw herself into her work. Michael told Janice that he expected to see her visit with the kids at least twice a year, that he and Diana would come up to Colorado for ski trips in the winter and for fly fishing in the summer.

Michael took over the insurance on the 280SL from his mom. He called his insurer, but they would not issue him a policy because the 280SL was considered a "vintage automobile." They referred Michael to a company that specialized in insuring older and collectible cars. When they wrote Michael a policy and he received the confirmation email, he was shocked to learn that the replacement cost on the 280SL was $250,000. Michael was overwhelmed. He knew it was worth something, but he had no idea that his dad's old car had appreciated so much. *Dad, you have always looked out for me. I guess that's true even now. Thank you*, Michael thought. Michael decided that he would drive the 280SL only on rare occasions.

CHAPTER 43

In early June, Isaac came home. Michael drove out to Hickam to pick up his brother. Michael saw Isaac get off the plane. Michael gave him a *Maile Lei*. They hugged. Isaac said, "Man, it's good to see you."

Michael said, "You look good—you shaved your beard."

Isaac said, "I couldn't wait to shave that fucker. It was always itchy. It was almost all gray, too."

Michael said, "That's why I don't grow beards anymore. I look like an old man." Michael asked his brother where he wanted to go for dinner.

Isaac said, "I want a big steak from Buzz's. I have been dreaming about that place for the past few months."

Michael said, "You got it." Michael told his brother how Buzz's had become the special-event-celebration place, that he was glad that Isaac had picked it. They sat down and immediately ordered two Hinanos.

Between sips, Michael asked his brother, "When are you going back to the '*Stan*?"

Isaac looked at his beer bottle and said, "Actually, I think I'm done with going back there. When I deployed this last time, I figured it was my last time."

Michael said, "Hmm."

Isaac continued, "It has been an incredible privilege and honor to serve my country in Afghanistan, but Special Operations is a young guy's world, and I can keep up, but barely. Now, pain actually *hurts*. It didn't before. I am getting a little tired of kicking in doors. I would do anything to keep my guys alive, but I'm thinking it's time for a younger SARC to take over."

This was a candid admission from a guy Michael always revered as being indestructible. Michael said, "Would you leave the Navy? You've only been in 16; you will get something in retirement, but you probably won't get a pension."

Isaac downed his Hinano and waved at the bartender for another for him and his brother. He said, "I would like to stay in the Navy. The Navy has been very good to me. If I have to take sick call on some ship somewhere, that would be alright. I've done it before."

Michael said, "That sounds like an incredible waste of your skill set, brother. You know more about trauma management than most surgical residents."

They both drank their beers in silence for a few minutes.

Then Michael said, "I think we're going to have to talk to a particular Navy Captain currently deployed at Landstuhl. Don't do anything until I hear back from her. You have some time. Let's see what Diana says."

When they left Buzz's, there were six empty bottles of Hinano on the table.

Michael drove the short distance to his mom's house. Sarah was waiting for them when they came in. Sarah and Isaac hugged.

Sarah told Isaac, "It's so good to see you."

Isaac said, "I missed you, mom. I miss dad every day, but that's different. When I'm there, I miss all of you."

Sarah said, "I'm sure that you're exhausted after your flight, and I'm going to bed. I have an early morning tomorrow. But I'm so glad that you're home." Sarah went off to her bedroom.

Michael and Isaac turned on the TV and were able to catch the last innings of the Dodgers playing in LA. Isaac fell asleep watching TV, and Michael woke him up when he went to bed a few hours later.

Michael arose early the next day and saw his brother awake, watching the morning news.

Michael said, "What the hell are you doing up? You should be asleep."

Isaac said, "My internal clock is all fucked up, I have no idea what time it is. Besides, I fell asleep around 10:30, and I woke up at 4, so I'm not really that tired."

Michael said, "Want to go surfing? I've been thinking about surfing with you for a long time."

Isaac said, "Absolutely."

A rare off-season low-pressure system in the Pacific was gifting the island with big waves. The North Shore was coming in at 8–10 feet, so they loaded up their long boards on the roof of the G63 and drove north for the hour-or-so drive to Waimea Bay, listening to the Bob Marley CDs that Diana had given Michael for Hanukkah. Both were singing along at the top of their lungs. They stopped for breakfast and coffee at the Haleiwa Coffee Gallery on the way.

Michael and Isaac got in a few really great sets. They were dialed in to the waves. Isaac got a tube. Eventually, so did Michael.

Michael was really happy to be surfing with his brother. Michael got tired and paddled in. He sat on the beach and watched his brother. He loved to watch his brother surf. It was the most natural and energetic thing he was fortunate to ever see. As a kid, Michael would often emulate Isaac's surfing style. Today, watching Isaac brought back all kinds of memories of the two of them growing up, of his dad, who used to take Isaac to all of his surf contests before Isaac could drive, of his mom, who used to cheer on Isaac every time he would shred a wave in a contest, even though no other contestants had mothers who did this. Michael thought about his sister, who wanted to learn to surf so badly. Isaac took her out on several occasions, but she never really got the hang of the sport. Michael thought about his beautiful wife, whom he and Isaac had taught to surf one winter break in college, many years ago.

An hour later, Isaac paddled in and put his board in the sand next to his brother's and sat down.

Isaac said, "Killer day."

Michael said, "*So killer.* I love watching you surf, man—always have."

Isaac said, "I'm the happiest when I'm in the water. I think that I want to be buried out there when my time comes."

Michael said, "Hopefully, that will be many years from now. I just buried our dad. Losing you, too, would make me very sad."

Isaac said, "I have been thinking about him so much lately, how fortunate we were to have him as a dad. I mean, I had a biological dad, but I don't really remember him. Joshua loved me like I was his own. He was always proud of me, even when I didn't do so well in school or when I got caught fighting after school."

Michael said, "He was good like that."

Isaac said, "Yep."

Michael said, "Me, too. Mom is thrilled that you're back, and so is Diana. She loves you."

Isaac said, "I love her, too. You finally found yourself. You look happy. First time in a long time I've seen you like this. I'm happy for you. You're going to be a great judge. Dad would be proud."

Michael said, "Thank you, brother."

Isaac, drawing a circle in the sand with his fingers, asked Michael, "Have you visited dad yet?"

Michael said, "Yes. I go up there once a month and sit in front of his grave and talk to him—it's comforting. I talk to Grandma and Grandpa, too."

Isaac said, "I want to start doing that, as well. I want to start visiting my birth parents' graves again, too." Joshua used to take Isaac to visit his father's grave periodically until one day Isaac told Joshua that he didn't want to see the graves anymore. That was years ago.

Michael told his brother, "You should. It's your connection to your past, to the people who brought you into this world."

CHAPTER 44

That night, when Michael had his daily call with Diana, he told her about Isaac.

Diana said, "Operators like Isaac have a finite shelf life before injuries set in. I have seen a lot of guys in Isaac's shoes. In the end, most of them just retire. There have been calls to give them special retirement incentives because of their hazardous-duty assignments. Remember the SEAL who apparently got Bin Laden? He left the SEALS with very few benefits. It's sad what the military does to those guys when they are no longer needed. They're the tip of the spear, and among the brightest, most capable members of the Armed Forces I have ever served with."

Michael said, "He wants to stay in the Navy. He told me that he would be happy taking sick call on some ship somewhere. He is a Senior Chief. I think he can do better than that."

Diana said, "You're so right—Isaac can do better, and his timing is perfect. I think I have something for him. Tripler just got a $250 million DOD grant to build the largest simulation lab in the Pacific Region. It will be state of the art. It will have mock-ups of shipboard trauma bays, field hospitals, and the exact replica of the inside of a Blackhawk. It will have high-tech mannequin patients that can simulate a wide variety of injuries. There will actually be an artificial battlefield where we can train on trauma management. They will be able to run multiple concurrent traumas. Every room will be wired with HD closed-circuit TV. Everything will be monitored by some of the best trauma specialists in the business. There will be training classrooms. The Army, Navy, and Air Force want to use it to expose newly minted corpsmen and medics who deploy to real-world situations that they would not normally see until they go down-range."

Michael said, "I would love to see this place sometime. When is it going to open?"

Diana said, "They just broke ground in an area that used to be the *Ewa* parking deck. They are going to reconfigure it for the trauma training center. The plan is for the center to open by the end of the year. I think Isaac would be perfect to run it. This job would not just be administrative—it would be hands-on as well. Isaac could train the next generation of corpsmen and medics heading down range. It would be a great testament to his legacy, and he would be really helping out the Navy. I bet if he asks really nicely, he can still do his dive medicine at Pearl."

Michael said, "What are the next steps?"

Diana said, "This isn't like judge shit, Michael. Isaac doesn't need Senate confirmation. He just has to tell me that he's interested, and we'll take care of the rest. It would be the perfect job for him, and he could easily stay in to get his 20, and he would be home."

Michael said, "Let me talk to him."

By the weekend, Isaac was getting up at dawn. Michael was up, too, and they walked the beach. Isaac ran into the ocean and dove in. Michael followed him. Michael got out and sat on the beach and waited for Isaac. They went and got coffee. Michael told Isaac about Diana's proposition and said, "I think it would be a great fit for you, and you have an incredible amount of knowledge that you could transfer to young, green corpsmen and medics who are heading off to war. But it would be different from what you have been doing for a while. Are you okay with that?"

Isaac sat there for a minute and said, unequivocally, "Yes. I'm in."

Michael shook his brother's hand and said, "Think about it—you could live at home, ride the Harley to Tripler every day, have your pick of just about any nurse in that place."

Isaac sat on the trunk of an old palm tree that had fallen, staring off at the sea, and said, "Hmm. I love the Harley, but I think I'll need a truck. I want a Tundra. The best thing about deploying is that you are too busy to spend money. I have a nice little chunk saved up."

Michael said, "Well *she-it*, brother. Let's go buy you a truck!"

Michael took Isaac into town, and Isaac bought a TRD Tundra Pro in Quicksilver, completely loaded. Isaac had gone to school with the general manager, and he gave Isaac the very best deal he could offer.

Two days later, Diana's brand-new G63 was delivered to the Grand house. Michael parked it right next to his and smiled at the sight of both of the big trucks parked next to each other.

In the end, transferring to Tripler wasn't that simple. It took a few months of wrangling between the Navy and Marines, and Isaac had to fly back to Pendleton to technically process out and fill out a ton of paperwork, and fly back and fill out a ton of more paperwork on the Tripler side, but the job was Isaac's. Isaac said that he thought that his dad was watching over him and that he had arranged for Isaac to get the job. Michael said that he felt like his dad had done the same thing for him. Sarah was thrilled that one of her children had moved back home and that two others were right down the street.

On a sunny Aloha Friday, Michael took his packed lunch to the pavilion on the grounds of Iolani Palace for lunch, sat on the grass, and watched the Royal Hawaiian Band play, as they do every Friday. After lunch, Michael walked over to Marvin's office and met with Amy Chong, one of the firm's family lawyers who also specialized in adoptions, to begin the long process of adopting a child. Diana and Michael had FaceTimed about this subject at great length, and Diana had warmed to the idea. Both were eager to take the first step, and both knew that it could take years to finally see it through.

One early morning when Michael was driving to work, he thought that his dad was always the connective tissue that held the family together. Joshua would give guidance, would always be there for his kids and Sarah, and they always knew that he loved them. When Joshua died, the family fell apart, but Joshua also brought them back together. Over time, Michael realized that he had stepped into the role of keeping the family together, that he wasn't forgetting his dad but paying tribute to him in the most ultimate way possible.

On a pretty September moonlit evening, the C-17 carrying Diana landed and taxied almost up to his car. Michael watched as soldiers, sailors, and airmen disembarked from the side door and down a stairwell on the large transport plane. His wife was the last to deplane. They hugged and kissed, and Michael gave Diana a beautiful double-strand orchid-and-*pikake* lei.

Michael said, "What, the Navy Captain had to sit in the rear of the plane?"

"No, they let the Navy Captain *stretch out* in the rear. I was able to sleep for almost the entire flight. The Ambien helped."

Michael said, "I'm glad you're home. Talking to you on the phone is not the same."

Diana said, "Right back at you, lover boy. I'm starving. Let's go eat." They hugged and kissed.

Michael grabbed Diana's bags and loaded them into the back of the G63. Michael said, "Can you wait until Kailua? We can go to Buzz's."

Diana said, "You have no idea how long I have wanted to go to Buzz's to have dinner with my husband."

Michael drove off and said, "Buzz's it is."

Buzz's wasn't crowded, and they were able to sit in a nice, quiet table and talk. Diana ordered a steak. Michael ordered the teriyaki chicken. They split a bottle of pinot noir. Diana said, "I missed this place. I missed us. I missed Sarah, and Isaac, and Janice. I missed sleeping in your small bed. I missed the way that you smell. I missed how you always clap your flip-flops together three times before you put them on your feet after we walk the beach. I missed the wood-fired hot tub and our talks in bed. I am the most fortunate person."

Michael reached over and kissed his wife. After dinner, Michael drove Diana to their new home. It was largely complete, and they would move in within the month. Earlier in the week, the Wolf professional stove and the Subzero refrigerator had been installed in the kitchen. The hot tub had been installed a few hours earlier. The landscapers had created a beautiful painting, with tropical plants and new trees.

241

Michael pulled into the dark driveway, his headlights illuminating their new house. It was beautiful—like a house left over from the 1930s, even though it was brand new. They got out of the G63.

Diana started crying.

Michael grabbed Diana's hand and said, "*Hey, what are you crying about?* This is a good thing."

Diana said, "I know. It is. Everything came together. Life is good, and I have nothing to complain about."

Michael said, "We are going to have a nice life. Here, check this out." Michael grabbed a flashlight that was sitting near the base step, and he led her up the side stairwell to the second-floor lanai and stood in front of what would be their bedroom. Michael said, "Look at the view." From their house, they could see many stars circling overhead. Michael continued, "If you listen hard enough, you can hear the ocean. You can see it during the day from up here. This will be our sanctuary from the world. The crazy world will be beyond the driveway. When we enter the house, we don't have to think about that until we leave for work the next day. I think we are going to have some nice memories in this house."

Diana just stood there, holding Michael's hand and staring at the stars.

ACKNOWLEDGEMENTS

ike Michael Grand, I am truly blessed to be surrounded by friends and family, many of whom offered to help with this book. I am eternally grateful to: George DeCesare, Rosemary Posner, Brad Spiegel, Isabel Hochhaus, Ed Novak, Erin Goff, Santina Bombaci, Steve Beeler, Mike Conroy, Dyan Cherry, Ralph Swan, Jeff Palencia, Wade Haras, Adam Posner, Ilona Babinsky.

Special thanks to: Alan Kelly, who was the very first reader of my first rough draft and encouraged me to continue on with the process. Rachel Wallach and Leah Hill gave unconditional love and support. Whitey Inga graciously read an earlier version. Vicki Wallach, who read each version of the manuscripts line-by-line, gave me great advice, and made me proud to have her be my mom. Elizabeth Farhart was an early reader who offered me advice on how to make the manuscript flow better. Dr. Kim Olson-Gibbs reviewed the manuscript and made sure that all the medical terminology and procedures were accurate, and that no patients were harmed in kitchen surgical procedures. Doug DeChance offered me inspiration and encouragement befitting of a good friend and showed me the true lesson of "surrender." David

Hill was one of the early readers of the manuscript. We talked for hours about what the book meant to him, and his comments found their way into subsequent drafts. Ira Berkowitz reviewed an early draft and pushed me to make it better. Then, he did it again on a subsequent draft. Bill Johnson gave me expert advice, both tactical and metaphysical. Ben Giacchino provided expert wine consultation that went directly into the book. I was privileged to have Jim Dannenberg watch me grow up and become a mentor to me when I eventually graduated from law school. He was kind enough to help with some of the aspects of being a judge in Hawaii. Gabe Hartman read an early version of the book and liked it so much that he had his wife, Faye, read it. Ruby Privateer gave me guidance that only a professional editor and a friend since college could. Last but not least, all of the amazing people at 1106 Design. I gave them a manuscript and they gave me a book.

Mahalo Nui Loa,
Jonathan Wallach, August 2018

The people in *The Speed of Water* are fictionalized based on several close friends and family members. Any attempt to identify them is strictly coincidental. The places in *The Speed of Water*, including the restaurants, are real. Next time you visit Oahu, visit some of them. You won't be disappointed.

GORUCK (www.Goruck.com) and Peacemaker Trading are real (www.bisonunion.com). Both truly are really cool companies run by some great people.

ABOUT THE AUTHOR

Jonathan Wallach grew up in Hawaii. He went to college in Boston and law school in Denver. He has spent his career studying privacy and data security laws and regulations. *The Speed of Water* is Jonathan's first novel.

45681507R00152

Made in the USA
Columbia, SC
22 December 2018